Studying on weekends is not one of life's greatest pleasures. Especially if you happen to know that just a few miles away your friends are having an overnight party without you.

Kristie had invited me, of course, but I had already promised to baby-sit Matthew. Just thinking about it made my head hurt, so I tried not to. I was also a tiny bit angry at my brother. I tried not to think about that, either.

The Victoria Mahoney Series
by Shelly Nielsen

#1 Just Victoria
#2 More Victoria
#3 Take a Bow, Victoria
#4 Only Kidding, Victoria
#5 Maybe It's Love, Victoria
#6 Autograph, Please, Victoria

AUTOGRAPH, PLEASE, VICTORIA

Shelly Nielsen

Chariot Books
DAVID C. COOK PUBLISHING CO.

A White Horse Book
Published by Chariot Books,
an imprint of David C. Cook Publishing Co.
David C. Cook Publishing Co., Elgin, Illinois
David C. Cook Publishing Co., Weston, Ontario

AUTOGRAPH, PLEASE, VICTORIA

Cover illustration by Gail Roth
First printing, 1987
Printed in the United States of America
92 91 90 89 87   5 4 3 2 1

Library of Congress Cataloging-in-Publication Data

Nielsen, Shelly, 1958—
    Autograph, please, Victoria.

    (The Victoria Mahoney series ; #6) (A White horse book)
    Summary; Junior-high-age Victoria learns to deal with
a young brother's learning disability, wins a writing
contest, and remembers that God loves people just the way
they are.
    [1. Conduct of life—Fiction] I. Title. II. Series:
Nielsen, Shelly, 1958-   . Victoria Mahoney series ; #6.
PZ7.N5682Au 1987   [Fic]   87-8854
ISBN 1-55513-216-2

for
Carolyn W.
Pam P.
Gwen L.
Mary G.
Karen E.
and Tammy H.
... wherever they are

1

"Matthew!"

Mom stood at the banister and called upstairs in an aggravated voice. Normally her face is pretty relaxed. She has this ear-to-ear grin that doesn't stop. At the moment, though, she looked life she might explode if someone just pushed the right button. There was a thin wrinkle between her eyebrows, and her hands were on her hips.

"If you're not down here in five seconds flat, I'll—Well, you're going to be sorry!"

I slouched against the front door with my backpack hooked over one shoulder, my coat buttoned, and my gloves on. I was ready to roll, but instead I was hanging around, waiting for my little brother to show up. He was always late getting ready for school. This is not good. Even in the first grade, teachers can be touchy about tardiness.

Upstairs Matthew's footsteps pounded as he raced around his room. Something crashed. "What was *that?*" Mom yelled.

"Nothing," Matthew called back sheepishly. "Just something breaking."

Mom put her hand to her head. "Probably the goldfish bowl," she said. "Victoria, what's going on? Why does your brother seem to be so much trouble lately?"

I shrugged. I didn't have a clue. Matthew really *was* a problem. A big one, considering he was such a young kid.

"I'd better go up," Mom said with a sigh. "Don't move. I'll be right back."

She climbed the stairs. Within a minute she came back down, holding my brother firmly by one arm.

"I'm disappointed," she was saying. "After all the promises you made yesterday. Remember when you said you'd hurry and be on time in the mornings? I thought I could depend on you."

Matthew's mouth drooped; his footsteps dragged. This kind of talk always gets a kid right where he lives. (It still gets to me, and I'm thirteen.)

"I'm sorry," he said.

Mom helped him into his coat while I opened the front door.

"Let's go," I said, prodding him outside. "We're

gonna be late, Matthew, old buddy. Hop to."

Another school day.

Matthew sat up front, and I climbed in back. I like having the back seat to myself. I can spread out, put my feet up on the seat, if I want. Sometimes I pretend I'm a famous writer being chauffeured around New York City.

Actually, Minneapolis doesn't look anything like New York, especially now that the piles of Thanksgiving snow were beginning to build around driveways. Our car crunched down the road toward school, every so often passing a snow bird. In Minnesota, "snow bird" refers to a car that hasn't been moved from its parking space on the street. After a winter storm the plows just come by and plow around it, burying the car and leaving only a huge mound of white. The owner probably doesn't see the car again until June.

Mom pulled the car into the Lonsdale Elementary parking lot, and my brother and I jumped out. My school, Keats Junior High, was just across the field.

"Bye, Mom." I thumped on the windshield and moved my mouth slowly so she could read my lips.

She rolled down her window. Her face was back to its old self. Under the pulled-down ski cap her brown eyes and pale-but-pretty Minnesota skin glowed. "Have a sensational, fun-filled day."

Matthew and I rolled our eyes. It's almost impossible to have a sensational school day. Parents sometimes forget this.

9

"And you have a terrific day at work," I said back. That got her; she wrinkled up her nose at me, gave a little toot on the horn, and drove away. Matthew and I trudged off to school.

"Hey, kid," I said as he veered off toward the elementary school entrance. "Tomorrow, why don't you try to be on time? Mom's not always going to be around to give you free chauffeur service, you know."

He bunched up his shoulders and shrugged. Then he turned and headed toward the front door, a very small kid even in all his bulky winter gear.

My best friend, Chelsie Bixler, was waiting for me at my locker. "You're late!" she said, without even a normal "Hi, how are you?"

Chelsie always meets me on Wednesdays, instead of walking to school with me, because she has glee club that morning. This day she looked a little tired, especially around the eyes. Sometimes I like to rub in the fact that I'm still asleep on Wednesdays while she's singing away.

"I would have been here sooner," I explained, "but I was in the middle of a huge family crisis."

Her eyes got wide, and her face brightened up. Chels loves a good story. "Tell me all the gory details."

I explained everything on the way to class. "Matthew's acting funny. It's mysterious. This morning he was late getting ready for school—again! He's also extremely grouchy when he gets home from school, and— Just a lot of things."

"He's just acting like a kid," Chels said. "Kids are supposed to act funny. All the ones I baby-sit act mighty peculiar. Last night, for instance, Monica Edwards and her brother Mark spray-painted their mother's scheffelera plant when I wasn't looking. Metallic gold. Not an attractive sight, let me tell you. Yessirree, Matthew sounds perfectly normal to me."

"You're probably right." I thought about Matthew's temper tantrums and how he suddenly hated school. He hadn't gotten one little smiley face at the top of a paper yet. His teacher always wrote comments like: "Try harder."

"Don't worry so much," Chelsie said. She likes to give me advice. "Save your worries for stuff like the writing contest."

"Why should I worry about that? I'd forgotten all about it."

She slapped her hand to her head. "You forgot about it?" she said, giving me a shake. "You *forgot* that you participated in the biggest writing contest of the year? Of the whole decade? Maybe even the century?"

"Cut it out," I said. "It was just a little contest."

"A *national* contest," she corrected me.

She unzipped her purse and dug around inside, pressing her books to her side. "Here," she said, handing me something. "I wanted to give you this.

11

It's a lucky writer's pen. Madeleine L'Engle used it to sign my copy of *A Wrinkle In Time* when she was at Byron's Bookstore."

"Wow." I looked it over and tested the button a couple of times.

"When do you find out who won the contest, o, mighty writer friend?"

"I don't know. A couple of weeks, maybe."

"Don't sweat it. You're the best writer I know—besides Madeleine L'Engle, of course."

I put my nose in the air. "Naturally," I said with a haughty half-smile. Then I laughed, my face going pink and tingly. It was embarrassing even to *pretend* being stuck up. "See you at lunch," I said, and waved.

2

As usual, Chels met me after school for the walk home. Outside it was too cold to talk much. We just scrunched our heads down into our scarves and walked fast.

"I'm moving to California," Chelsie said as we hurried along. "I am very thin-blooded, and all this cold weather isn't good for my metabolism." Chels likes to flash big words around. I made a mental note to look up *metabolism* when I got home.

Just then a sporty car pulled alongside us. The passenger-side window rolled down. "Hello!"

"Ms. Runebach-Dahl," Chelsie and I said together. She's an English teacher at Keats, and an old friend of ours.

13

She motioned toward the back seat. "Can we give you a lift?"

"Great," said Chels. "We're frozen."

Chelsie scooted across the seat, and I got in after her, noticing that Ms. Runebach-Dahl's husband was driving. He teaches health at our school. I don't know him that well, but Chelsie had him for a health class, so she gave him directions to our houses. I can be shy in situations like this.

Ms. Runebach-Dahl twisted around and looked right at me.

"Are you getting excited about the contest?" she asked. "They'll be notifying winners pretty soon." She turned to her husband and explained, "Victoria was one of three Keats students who wrote essays in the National Scholastic Contest."

I hadn't really thought about it that much, but I didn't want to say so. It would probably hurt her feelings.

When I didn't pipe right up, she said, "You're not *nervous*, are you?"

"Not exactly," I said, but I wasn't sure. I *had* been feeling pretty relaxed, but with everybody bringing it up all the time, I was starting to get the jitters.

"What was your essay about?" Mr. Runebach-Dahl asked over his shoulder. He had a nice voice. I also noticed that he was growing a beard. When men start growing beards they look pretty scruffy. I didn't say so, of course.

"It was about individuality," I said instead.

14

"Fascinating," he said. "So how'd you get to be an expert on that topic?"

I didn't know what to say. Chels gave me a pinched, proud little smirk.

"Well," I said, starting to ramble, which I have been known to do, "I guess partly because I'm a Christian. Christians are usually a little different from everyone else . . . on account of their beliefs and stuff."

"Oh?" he said.

I kept talking. "Also, I have some pretty unusual relatives. At least that's what everyone tells me."

"Tell me about them," he said. "My relatives are so normal they'd bore you to tears. I'd love to have some unusual relatives."

Everybody was waiting, so I started in, sort of embarrassed. "Well, my dad used to be a hippie. You know, with long hair and love beads and every thing, but now he's so clean-cut, you wouldn't believe it."

"Very clean-cut," said Chels, nodding.

"His name's Terry, and he's a chef at a restaurant called 'F. Scott's' after F. Scott Fitzgerald, who was a famous writer from Minnesota." Then I stopped, horrified. Of course they knew who F. Scott Fitzgerald was. They were *teachers*, for crying out loud.

"That's an excellent restaurant," said Ms. Runebach-Dahl, skipping right over the F. Scott comment. "I always get the shrimp scampi."

"—And my mom, Bobbi," I said, "is a counselor

at a senior citizens' home, and she's into health foods. She's practically a fanatic. And I have a grandmother who doesn't like to be called Grandma. We have to call her Isadora. Her hair is sometimes white, and sometimes red, depending on her mood and whether she has recently dyed it. She just got married to my new grandfather, Mr. Wilkes, over Thanksgiving. I could tell you wild stories about their wedding, but it would probably take a year. They don't believe in any of that traditional wedding march and candleabra stuff."

"I guess you are an expert on individuality," said Mr. Runebach-Dahl. "Must have been a great essay."

By now we were pulling up at my house. I gathered up my stuff.

"Thanks," I said. "Thanks a lot."

"Don't mention it," said Mr. Runebach-Dahl.

All three of them waved at me as they pulled away.

3

Mom, Matthew, and I were traveling the familiar roads to the restaurant. Sometimes we go to F. Scott's to have dinner with Dad. It's fun. Along the way, the Christmas shoppers were already out—bundled-up figures carrying bags and peering into the decorated display windows. I could hardly believe it was Christmastime already. Time goes by faster, the older you get.

Things looked slow at F. Scott's. A few people glanced up from their food as we passed the picture window. Plenty of empty tables. Good. That meant Dad would have time for a break.

I felt the usual flush as we pushed through the big oak doors of the restaurant. You couldn't help feeling elegant here. The maitre d', wearing an ironed white shirt and creased black pants, swept up to us.

"A pleasant evening, Mrs. Mahoney," he gushed.

"Oh, Howie. Call me Bobbi, remember?" My mom is very down-to-earth.

Howie blushed. "Of course. Let me show you to a table. Mr. Mahoney—Terry—said you'd be stopping."

In a secluded corner, he pulled out a chair for Mom. Matthew and I scooched our own chairs in. My brother stuffed his face into the flowers and sniffed. Next he tried to hold his hand over the candle.

"Yow!" he said, yanking his hand back. I rolled my eyes. So much for elegance.

"Dinner?" Howie asked, raising his eyebrows.

"Yes," said Mom, "I think Terry's going to whip up something simple for us."

"Excellent." He rushed off in the direction of the kitchen.

"*I'm* impressed," I said. "Are *you* impressed?"

Mom grinned. "Very. Who'd have thought the thrifty Mahoneys could fit in at such a classy place?"

In a second, Dad came out of the kitchen, looking official in white. "Sauce maltaise," he said, pointing to a stain on his apron. "Delicious; wait and see." He took the empty seat. "How was school, offspring?" he asked, leaning forward with his hands under his chin.

"This is going to be a devastating blow," I told

him. "School was boring—as usual. Nothing new to report."

"Bor-ing," Matthew agreed.

"Oh, come on. I arranged this impromptu dinner here at a high-class restaurant, and you don't have any juicy stories?"

"Like when do you hear about the two-hundred-dollar prize?" Matthew asked me, his eyebrows doing loop-de-loops. "Hmm?"

Everyone laughed. He only remembered the prize money, probably, because in a weak moment I had promised to share with him if I won it.

"What *is* this?" I asked. "Everybody's always talking about the contest. I'm a nervous wreck."

Mom flapped open her napkin and smoothed it over her lap. "Don't worry. You don't have to win. Just participating in the contest was honor enough." Mothers like to say stuff like this.

"I just hope you don't have your hearts set on my winning," I said. "It's a national contest, after all."

"We'll try to keep a sense of proportion," said my father. "Hey, I'm starved. You guys feel like some grub? Let's see what I can scare up."

After Howie himself carried out the dinners, we bowed our heads over the steaming plates, and Matthew prayed—a little too loudly, if you ask me. Then we dug in.

We were all talking a mile a minute and laughing and interrupting each other when Howie whisked by, directing a young couple to the table behind us.

Suddenly our conversation dropped off. I knew what was wrong. The people had a little sleeping baby with them.

Not even a year ago, something happened that changed everything in our family. Our baby died. She wasn't even supposed to be born until a month later, but one day Mom's doctor said the baby's heart wasn't beating. Mom went to the hospital. When the baby was delivered, she wasn't breathing. She wasn't alive. The baby's name was Jessica.

Finally getting up the nerve, I swallowed and looked at my parents. Mom had forked her food into neat piles on the plate. Dad smiled weakly at me and started talking again. But his eyes kept sneaking looks over at the baby. After a stillbirth, things are never the same, no matter how hard you try.

4

"This is stupid," I called.

But Chelsie was yards ahead of me; I don't think she heard. Or maybe she was just ignoring me. It was afternoon, and the school had cleared out, but she was still galloping down the echo-y hallway.

"Why are you walking so fast?"

"I told you," she said, making a quick right and vanishing.

I whipped around the corner where she had disappeared. She was waiting for me. She had flattened herself against the wall like some sort of movie detective or something.

"I told you," she repeated in a whisper. "Because you wore the same outfit I wore today. Anybody who gets a good look at us will think we're identical twins or something."

"*Accidentally* I wore the same outfit."

We both looked down at our clothes. I had on shiny black loafers, grey denims, and my favorite plaid shirt. Looking at Chels was like looking in a mirror, except that she had rolled up her sleeves and changed into tennis shoes.

"I *know* it was an accident," she said in a patient voice. "But I can't help it; I still feel like an idiot."

"Anyway," I pointed out. "The coast is clear now."

She peered around. "Yeah, you're right. Finally." She breathed out a relieved sigh. "Look, I'm sorry for avoiding you all day. I mean, who cares what everyone thinks? Right?" Turning, she began whirling the combination on her locker. I raced her, but she got hers open first, because mine always sticks.

"Come over to my house," I said, dumping my science book into the mess of papers in the bottom of the locker. I dug for my math book. "It's boring baby-sitting Matthew, and Mom and Dad won't get home for hours. You could help me find something exciting to do. That is, if you're not too humiliated to be seen with me."

She screwed up her face at me.

Just then a stampede of flat-footed tennis shoes came clomping down the hall. It was Peter and his gang of weird-o friends. Peter is a friend of mine, but when he is with his friends, he's different. Like a regular old Dr. Jekyll and Mr. Hyde.

"Hey," he said, squeaking to a stop and pointing at us. "Who're you two supposed to be? The Bobbsey Twins?"

I didn't know who the Bobbsey Twins were, but I went purple anyway. Chels made a fierce face.

"Oh, go eat it, Peter," she said.

Peter laughed and his friends laughed and then they ran again, leaving us standing there in the hallway.

"I probably shouldn't have said that," she told me. "It wasn't very Christian."

"Probably not," I agreed.

We slammed our locker doors and headed toward home.

It was a quiet walk, except that near my house a snowball hit the sidewalk in front of us with a splat.

"Hey—!" I yelled, taken by surprise.

My brother pranced toward us. "Mom and Dad are going to schoo-ool," he sang.

"What?"

"They're gonna meet my teacher. Mr. Crawford invited 'em."

At that same instant, Mom and Dad came out the front door. Mom was dressed in her usual work clothes (I could tell by the nylons and high heels showing beneath her long coat), and Dad had put on a jacket and a tie. They had serious looks on their faces, but when they saw us they smiled.

Dad called to us. "You wonderful young women

want to do us a colossal favor?"

"What?" I asked, skeptically.

"Baby-sit Matthew."

My brother howled. "I'm too old for baby-sitters."

"—*Entertain* Matthew, I meant," Dad said. "We have an appointment with his teacher."

"How come you're meeting with Mr. Crawford?" I said, walking toward them. "It's not parent-teacher conferences."

They looked embarrassed. Mom scraped her boots in the snow. "Just to talk a few things over," she explained, giving my hair a gentle tug. "We'll be back before you know it."

"And what're you doing off work so early?" I called after them as they moved toward the garage.

"We'll be back before you know it," Mom repeated. They got into the car, and we stood back to let it pass.

"Weird," I said, when they had disappeared with a gray puff of exhaust.

"I am?" Matthew said. He stopped rolling a huge snowball and looked at me with his frozen pink face.

"Not you, Matthew," I said, impatiently. "Mom and Dad."

"Oh. Good." He gave a shove to the snowball and it rolled over, lumpily.

"Hot cocoa time," Chelsie said wisely, tugging me by the sleeve toward the front door. "Let's go, Twin."

24

Later, while Mom drove Chelsie home, I helped Dad make some dinner. He was awfully quiet.

"How'd the meeting go?" I said, to break the ice.

"Oh, okay." He rinsed some fish filets in the sink. Then he looked up at me with a puzzled face. "Actually, it was strange."

"Well, any teacher who has a snake named Arnold has to be a little on the odd side," I pointed out.

"Actually, Mr. Crawford is the picture of normality, pet snake aside. Tonight he was wearing a gray wool suit coat and a very conservative tie. Mr. Crawford is decidedly un-strange. No, it's something else. Your brother is doing poorly in school."

"It takes time for little kids to get used to school, Dad. They're funny that way."

He crossed his arms. "Matthew's been to kindergarten, and he's in his fourth month of first grade."

"True." I bit my lip, thinking. "Well, maybe he's just feeling rambunctious." (Rambunctious is a word I learned from Isadora, and it fits my brother to a T.) "Chelsie baby-sits for kids who spray-paint house plants. Matthew may be peppy, but at least he doesn't spray-paint house plants."

Dad dried his hands on the towel and stood leaning against the sink, looking uncomfortable in his dressy clothes. "No, he doesn't do stuff like that. But Mr. Crawford says he's disruptive in class; he doesn't settle down. And he's not learning the things he's supposed to learn."

"Like what?"

25

"Spelling. Math. How to read," Dad answered. "And simple interactive skills."

I didn't know what interactive skills were, but the rest made sense. "Sesame Street taught him his ABCs ages ago. And we're always reading to him."

Dad held his arms out in a helpless shrug. "I know. So how come Matthew's forgotten it all? Anyway, Mr. Crawford suggested we have a doctor check him out—to make sure he's *physically* okay."

My brother hollered from the family room where he was watching a roaring-loud TV. "What, Dad? Did you say something, Dad?"

Dad smiled a tired smile. "No. I'll call you when dinner's ready."

Then he sighed and turned back to the sink.

5

Janell Hornsby threaded some of her hot lunch peas through her hoop earrings, stuck the posts back in her ear holes, and went on eating as if nothing had happened.

"What?" she kept saying, flipping her head around. "Why are you all laughing? What's wrong?"

Luckily the lunchroom is a noisy place, because that made us scream with laughter. Peggy choked on her milk, and Chelsie had to pound on her back until Peg's face got red.

"Stop!" she yelled. "You're killing me!"

I clung to the edge of the table. "I've never . . . ever . . . laughed so hard," I gasped.

"Idiots," said Janell, tossing her head and taking an enormous bite of lasagne.

Finally we recovered enough to pick up our silverware again. Kristie studied a forkful of wilted parsley, turning it over and over. "That's what I like about all of you," she said. "You have such good manners. My mother would love you. You're so quiet and serious."

"Right," Janell said.

"—And you're lucky to have such wonderful friends," Chels pointed out. The laughter began to build again.

"—Because right at this moment," Peggy Hiltshire said, joining in, "I could be having lunch with Susie Laplorden and Jennifer Umber, and they're really popular. Not like you guys."

She meant it as a joke, but it came out wrong. The rest of us looked at each other.

"I was just kidding," Peggy said, giving me a shove. I bounced off of Janell, who kind of crashed into Chelsie. We barely managed a laugh, though; suddenly things didn't seem so funny. We went back to our lunches.

The quiet was pretty uncomfortable. After awhile Peggy stood up, clutching her lunch tray. "Guess I'll get going," she said. "See you all."

I watched her weave through the lunchroom crowd, noticing that a lot of people—guys included—said hi to her as she passed.

"Wonder where she's off to?" I said.

"Probably to find her *pop*-ular friends," said Kristie, crossing her eyes. "Excuse *me*."

"Well, I don't know about you," Janell said, "but I'm depressed. Sometimes Peggy lacks tact, know what I mean?"

"I don't think she meant it the way it sounded," said Chels.

Silence.

I raised my hand, as if I were in class.

"What is it, Ms. Mahoney?" Chelsie asked in an official voice.

"I have a question. A serious question."

"Shoot."

"What do you have to do to be popular? I mean *popular*."

"Simple," Kristie said. "Distribute five-dollar bills to everyone you meet."

"Look like a *Seventeen* model at all times," Chels added. "Even first thing in the morning."

"Act like one, too," said Janell. Suddenly she swept down over Chelsie's hand. "Oh, dahling!" she said, making smoochy noises. "You look divine."

Chelsie extended her hand stiffly, holding her pinky up high. "Dahling, you, too!" She held the pose for a couple of seconds, but finally she fell face-first into the table on her crossed arms, laughing hysterically.

"See, Vickie?" Janell spread her arms. "It's simple."

"No, really," I said. I can be very persistant. "Can

you become popular if you work at it?"

No one said anything. They shifted around for comfortable positions on their chairs.

"*You're* popular," Kristie said.

I squinted at her. I have this piercing look that melts iron. I've used it on my brother for years.

"Okay, you're popular *enough*," she said. "Maybe not popular like Peggy and Susie and Jennifer, but you're. . . ." Her face twisted as she tried to think of the right word. ". . . *you*," she said at last.

I shrugged. I guessed I wasn't going to get an answer out of them.

"Hey," said Chels, slurping the last bit of milk through her straw and turning to me. "Have you heard about the writing contest yet? Huh?"

I sighed. "I'd like to forget about the contest for awhile. You've mentioned it every day for the last two weeks."

Chelsie exhaled a huge exasperated breath. "Even if you *don't* care about winning, I do. I even asked Ms. Runebach-Dahl when she'd find out; she said any day now. The awards committee is real quick about the choosing the winners."

Kristie let out a squeal—"It'd be exciting if you really did win!"—and Janell leaned sideways. "Do you think you have a chance, kid? I always knew you were a terrific writer."

I shrugged. A self-conscious flush rose up my neck to the tips of my ears, followed by another sensation: a soft, unexpected glow of pride.

6

At breakfast, Mom reminded my brother that he had a doctor's appointment later that day. A frown started spreading across his face, and by the time Mom had brought in a plate of steaming toast, he was practically glaring. He hasn't trusted doctors since he stepped on a rusty nail and had to get a tetanus shot.

"I'm not sick," he said ferociously. "I don't need to go to the doctor."

Mom pulled up her chair and sat down. "It's only a check-up, Matthew," she said. "Everybody gets a check-up once in a while." She took a crunchy bite of toast.

I had to hand it to her; she was very low-key. In emergencies, she's good at this ho-hum attitude.

31

But Matthew wasn't fooled. "Little kids don't get check-ups," he said. "Only grown-up old people get check-ups."

My brother can be horribly logical. Even Mom looked surprised and didn't have anything more to say.

I stared at him, wondering why Mr. Crawford thought he needed a check-up. What if Matthew had a disease or something? That would be horrible. Every day we'd have to visit him in the hospital. He'd probably just lie in a big hospital bed looking pale and pathetic. I put another bite of oatmeal in my mouth and checked him over for signs of disease. He looked okay. His hands were a little dirty and his shirt was misbuttoned, but that was normal.

"Think of it this way," I pointed out. "When you go to the doctor, you get to skip school. Most kids will do anything to get out of school early. Today, for instance, we're having an assembly, and I'm overjoyed. Thrilled. One whole hour of freedom."

Matthew thought that over. Then the frown came back. "But I hate doctors!"

Mom and Dad peered at each other over their mugs.

"How about a bribe?" Dad asked at last. "Will you go if we bribe you?"

"Dad!" I said. "You're going to bribe your own kid? Dr. Spock would have a fit!"

"Hey," he said, "When *you're* a parent, you can go by the book if you want. In the meantime, I'm the dad, and I'm not above a bribe once in awhile. How about it, Matthew? Can I interest you in a deal?"

Matthew lowered one eyebrow. "What kind of deal?"

Just as the two of them settled on a Friday night of Cokes, popcorn, and a late movie, someone knocked on the door. I ran to answer it.

"Hi, gorgeous," Chelsie said. "Let's go."

"Hold on while I get my coat," I said, heading for the closet. "You ready?" I called to my brother. He tore past us and up the stairs. Sighing, I suited up for the walk to school.

"Do you mind if we wait for Matthew?" I said. "He's so disorganized, you wouldn't believe it. But I should probably make sure he gets to school okay."

"No problem."

We stood at the front door listening to his footsteps pounding overhead.

"If you're not down here in five seconds," I called, sounding like Mom, "I'm leaving. You can walk to school by yourself."

"I'm coming!"

Finally he appeared, puffing.

"Well?" I said. "Put on your coat."

He did.

"Where are your mittens?"

"I don't know."

For once, I couldn't keep the anger from creeping into my voice. I didn't care if he *did* have an incurable disease. "For goodness' sake, Matthew, go find them."

Chels and I looked at each other while he rummaged around in the hall closet.

"Little brothers," I whispered to her, rolling my eyes.

On the way to the school assembly I ran into Chelsie—really ran into her.

It wasn't my fault; the crowd was rowdy, and I kind of got shoved. Kids feel spunky when they get out of class for an hour.

"Youch," she said, rubbing her arm. "But as long as you're here, want to sit together?"

Janell joined us outside the auditorium. "What's this assembly all about?" she wanted to know. "Don't tell me the principal's going to talk about academic motivation again. I can't take it."

"It's an awards show," I told her. "They announced it over the intercom."

Chels groaned. "Dull, dull, dull," she said.

Janell stretched and yawned. "Maybe I'll get some shut-eye."

"Just don't snore," I said. "If you're planning to snore, could you please sit a couple rows ahead of us?"

We went into the dim auditorium and scrounged up three empty seats near the back.

It's amazing how many awards there are for people in junior high. There were spelling awards and math awards and art awards. After Mr. Brownsdale, the vice principal, described each achievement, he'd announce the winner, and everyone would clap while the person went up front. Description; name; applause. I fell into the routine.

Janell dropped her head back against her seat and made loud snoring sounds. Chelsie gave her a sharp elbow in the ribs.

"And now—" The microphone squealed as Mr. Brownsdale leaned too close. "Now," he said in a quieter voice, "a national award to one of Keats's very own students."

"I've got to rest," I whispered to Chels. "My hands are numb."

"—This goes to an unusually talented individual. From hundreds of junior high students across the nation, the judges have selected her work for second place. The prize is $125."

"Ooo," said the audience.

"The competition was the National Scholastic Writing Contest—"

I had begun to get a fizzy sensation in my stomach.

"—And the winning student is our own Victoria Mahoney. Victoria, would you come forward?"

Chelsie whipped around. "That's you!" she said. "Get going." She grabbed me hard by my arm and gave me a boost forward. I stumbled over the legs in the way and out into the aisle.

The applause lasted the long trip down to the

35

stage. I climbed the steps. The bright spotlights blinded me. Mr. Brownsdale was standing by the podium holding a certificate and extending his hand. I shook his hand, staring up at him. I'd never seen him that close.

"Unfortunately, we don't have the check yet," Mr. Brownsdale said, still clutching my hand and turning to the mike.

"Aww," came the chorus of voices.

"—But we'll forward it to Ms. Mahoney as soon as we do receive it."

He shook my hand for a few more seconds. Then I turned and climbed down the steps. The applause started up again. With the light dazzling me, I walked straight back to my seat—fast.

7

"There she is!" Chels said, pointing through the glass.

Sure enough. The old green bomb was pulling up into the school parking lot.

"Let's head 'em out," I said, motioning. We gathered up our books and went outside.

My brother was sprawled in back with his trucks, so Chels and I hopped up front, slamming the door. The darkness, the clean smell of Mom's cologne, and the soft hum of radio music surrounded us.

"Hi, o Mom-of-mine," I said, buckling up. "You're right on time."

"Thanks for inviting me, Mrs. Mahoney," said Chelsie. "I haven't been to a restaurant in ages."

"Would we celebrate a big event like this without you, Chelsie?" said my mom. It was a nice thing to say. Chels smiled and sat back.

We were on our way to a big dinner, in honor of my winning the contest. Kind of embarrassing, but pretty fun, too.

"Well? Well?" Mom asked as the car lurched into gear. "Tell me everything. Were you shocked when the principal called your name? What did he say? Did you have an acceptance speech ready? Were you brilliant?" She shot a quick look at me. "Why aren't you saying anything? You're not depressed, are you? Oh, no! It didn't go well. Did your mind go blank? Speak to me!"

"Mom, I can't get a word in."

"Oh. Sorry. Listen, you go ahead. I won't even open my mouth until you've given us the whole scoop. Look. My lips are zipped."

"Well, first thing—"

"Stop!" she shouted suddenly, stomping on the brakes as we came to a stop sign. "Don't say a word. We're picking up your father, and he'll be furious if he misses even one solitary detail. Save your stories for later."

"But—"

"Not one more word. Oh, this is exciting. I can hardly wait."

I folded my arms and tried to ignore the commotion Matthew was making in the back seat. I was tired out; the last thing I needed was to be bugged by my rowdy brother. When he leaned over the seat, I braced myself for a fight. But all he did was whisper in my ear: "Howdy."

My anger faded. Every once in a while a little brother can make you go soft and mushy. "Hi, kiddo," I whispered back.

"You could tell *me* about the assembly."

"Yeah, I guess I could," I said. I made my voice sound sort of light and teasing. "But on second thought, I think I'll make you wait, too."

"Aw," he said. But he leaned quietly back into his seat.

Outside of F. Scott's, Dad was waiting for us. "The whole night off!" he said, clearing some space in the back seat and sliding in. "Some events are too earth-shattering to let go by without wild merry-making. Let's party!"

Mom took off.

"The way I look at it," he said as we drove along, "our next step is selling the house and moving to Hollywood. That way Vickie can get started right away on her first award-winning screenplay."

"—In my elegant apartment overlooking the ocean," I said, grinning. "I like it."

The Gondola is practically my favorite restaurant in the world. It's Italian, and there's so much red everywhere, you wouldn't believe it. Also their manicotti is the greatest. Loads of garlic.

We stood clumped in the lobby. I had a funny

feeling—a dizzy, carnival-ride feeling. I guess the surprise of winning the contest was sinking in.

Finally we were shown to a table with a red-checkered table cloth. It was a very romantic table, the kind of table you wouldn't mind sitting at if you were on a real, honest-to-goodness date. But it was nice to be here with my family, too.

We all opened our menus. I held mine near the candle so I could read the prices. Wow. The food here was expensive.

I cleared my throat. "Um . . . listen, I'll be getting my check for $125 pretty soon. At which time I'll be loaded."

"Go ahead," Mom said. "Rub it in."

"No, what I mean is, I could pay you back for dinner tonight."

Dad gave my hand a pat. "We don't eat out much. On special occasions, I think your mother and I can handle it."

That's the kind of folks I have. "Thanks, Dad."

"Yeah, thank you, Mr. and Mrs. Mahoney," Chels said. She has manners like you wouldn't believe.

Matthew was leaning back in his chair. He leaned farther and farther back. Just as he was about to tip backwards, Mom jerked the chair forward so the legs hit the floor with a *thump*.

"Now behave," she told him.

He got whiney and fidgety, and finally, Dad told him to cut it out *now*.

40

Then Matthew spilled a whole glass of water on the tablecloth. It dripped into my lap. Slowly, ordinariness came back to the evening. My good mood was slipping away, like air seeping out of a balloon. Finally, I couldn't stand it anymore. "What's wrong with you?" I snapped. "Why can't you be good? Why can't you be quiet just one night?"

"Shut up," he said.

"Matthew!" Dad gave him a look of warning.

I turned to Mom. "Didn't the doctor tell why Matthew's such a brat?"

"Mom!" my brother howled.

I knew I shouldn't be talking about this stuff in front of Chelsie, but I was really angry.

Mom's voice was subdued. "Dr. Hamilton says Matthew's healthy as an ox."

"Then, how come—?"

"Victoria," Mom said. "We'll discuss it later." Her eyes, sparkling in the candlelight, were stern, and her shoulders were straight and square. To fill up the embarrassing quiet, I picked up my water glass and took a long drink.

"Now," Mom said after a moment, and her voice was back to its bright self. "Have you all decided what you're going to have? I'm starving."

"Well," Dad said, coming downstairs to the family room, where Mom and I were sitting. "Matthew conked out the instant his little head hit the pillow. He must have been exhausted."

41

"That figures," I said. "Acting like a jerk at a restaurant takes a lot of energy."

I heard Mom sigh heavily from the rocking chair. The evening had started out to be magical-wonderful, and Matthew had ruined it. I lifted Bullrush, my cat, onto my lap and stroked his warm fur. I have read that petting animals will lower your blood pressure. It was worth a shot.

Dad sprawled next to me. "We need to talk," he said.

"Okay."

"Bobbi?" Dad raised his eyebrows to Mom. "You want to summarize?"

"No. Yes. Okay. Well, first off—" She stopped. "I'm a nervous wreck. Vickie, can I borrow Bullrush for a sec?"

"Sure." I handed him over. He settled down in Mom's lap with his eyes slitted, and his wild purring filled up the room. Mom ran her hand over his orange back in time with the ticking of the wall clock. After a few moments she looked up.

"Dr. Hamilton says Matthew could have something called a learning disability."

"What's that?"

"I don't understand it all, but it means that he doesn't have the capabilities to learn in the same way that other children learn."

"You mean he's dumb?"

Her eyes grew fierce. "Not dumb. Just different."

Dad cut in. "A lot of kids have learning disabil-

42

ities. They have to work extra hard to learn some things, and their frustration sometimes causes discipline problems. I don't know, but maybe that has something to do with why he's been acting so crazy lately—even tonight in the restaurant."

"Next week," Mom continued, "we're going to meet with a learning disabilities specialist. She'll test Matthew's abilities and help us set up some kind of learning program. Oh, I don't want to talk about this anymore. It's depressing."

For the umpteenth time that night, I was surrounded by uncomfortable silence.

"I'm sorry," I said. Boy, was that a stupid thing to say.

Dad stuffed his hands into his pockets. "And I'm sorry about tonight. We wanted the evening to be special for you."

"It was," I said. "It really was." I put my arm around Dad's shoulder and kissed his cheek. Then I went over and kissed Mom. I decided to give Bullrush a smack, too, as long as I was at it.

"I'll try to be nicer to Matthew—at least until we find out what's wrong with him."

Mom looked relieved. "Would you? That would help."

She suggested that a prayer might be in order. We each prayed that God would take care of Matthew and help us be patient with him. Then Mom balanced the Bible on Bullrush's back and read a Psalm out loud, while Bullrush purred.

Afterward, Dad tapped my shoulder. "Have I told you lately how proud I am? About the contest?"

"Only about five or six times tonight. But who's counting?"

I climbed up the steps to my room—quietly, because I didn't want to wake my brother.

8

After your body gets used to the weekend, Monday morning feels about as nice as an icy shower. I was in my usual Monday a.m. daze, just kind of shuffling through the hallway toward my first class. Suddenly someone grabbed me and pulled me out of the crowd.

It was Ms. Runebach-Dahl. She took hold of both my arms and kind of hopped up and down. Considering she is normally very reserved, this was a real surprise. For a second I was speechless.

"I had to congratulate you," she said breathlessly. "I knew you'd win the writing contest. I knew it."

"I didn't *win*, exactly," I told her. "That girl in Pittsburgh got first."

"Good grief, Victoria," said Ms. Runebach-Dahl. "There you go again. When will you ever accept a compliment and acknowledge your achievements? You did a good job, and you deserve some acclaim."

She was right. It dawned on me like a flashlight shining in my face. I had won. I had done a good job. It felt good.

"Oh!" she said. "This reminds me. A reporter from the *Keats Crier* stopped by and wanted to know how to get in touch with you." Ms. Runebach-Dahl grinned. "I told her I knew the writer celebrity personally. I set up an interview for you after school tonight. How does that sound?"

"Okay, I guess. The Johnstons baby-sit Matthew until I get home from school, and they don't mind if I'm late once in a while. The Johnstons are our next door neighbors and—" I was babbling; I only babble when I'm nervous. Already I had stomach pains. An interview. I'd never been interviewed before.

"She said she'd be waiting in the newspaper office."

My heart was really going, now. I joined the crowd of kids on their way to first period.

That afternoon, I knocked firmly at Room 201.

"Yeah? Who is it!" came a voice through the door.

"Victoria Mahoney," I said, trying to sound dignified. "The writer."

Footsteps clattered. The door flew open.

"Hi," said the girl. "Remember me?"

It was my old friend, Melody McClure. We had taken a writing class together once, and I hadn't seen her around much since.

"I remember," I said, the knot in my stomach loosening. "Hi, Melody. You're a reporter now?"

She fluttered her mascara-ed lashes. "Sure. And I'm good, too—the best. Oh, rats! I think I lost a contact. Don't move!" She crouched down and felt around the floor. "Crumb, I can't see a thing." She cupped a hand over one eye, then the other. "No. Sorry, false alarm. Come on in."

I stepped in. The newspaper office was tiny, with no windows and hardly any room.

"Welcome to our little storage closet," Melody said. "It ain't much, but at least there's space for a table and a couple chairs. Sit down."

One thing about Melody—she was still wearing loads of make-up. Her eyelids sparkled, and her lips were a pearly pink that matched her cheeks. I couldn't decide if it was glamorous or strange; I'd have to think about it.

"Don't be nervous," she said. "Are you nervous?"

"A little."

"Look at it this way: the reporter is really the one under pressure; she's got to think up great questions. All you have to do is answer them."

Except I've got to think of snappy answers, I thought, but of course I didn't say it.

She uncapped a pen and whipped open her notebook. "Math notes," she explained, flipping past a couple of filled pages and finally reaching a blank sheet.

"Now." She chomped down on her pen. "When did you first know you wanted to be a writer?"

"For one thing, my Dad used to read Charles Dickens' books to me when I was a little kid. You know, like *Oliver Twist* and *Great Expectations*. He had this funny way of doing it. He made up a voice for every character. For instance, Oliver had a high squeaky voice. When the Artful Dodger had a line, Dad would put on this hat and use an English accent. The way my Dad reads stories is almost better than a movie. Anyway, that's when I started liking stories. I guess I always thought maybe someday I would write a novel and—"

"Wait a minute, wait a minute," Melody interrupted. Her pen was writing furiously. " 'My Dad used to read Charles Dickens. Then what?"

"Well, he read books like—"

"Hold it." She pulled open a filing cabinet and lugged out a cassette recorder which she placed on the table with a *thunk*.

"You're going to record me, Melody?"

"Yeah. You don't expect me to write as fast as you talk, do you?"

She pushed a couple of buttons; the cassette wheels turned. "That's better," she said, grinning. "Okay, start again."

"Um—" I looked at the recorder. My mind was a

giant blank. "What was the question again?"

"Oh, let's forget that one. It was boring. Let's talk about now. Where did you get the inspiration to write your award-winning essay?"

"Well, the prize money helped inspire me."

She looked at me. "Huh?"

"It was a joke, Melody. I was kidding."

"Oh. *Oh!* I like it. 'Brilliant writer still has time for laughs.' This will be a great article, kid."

9

"This interview is officially over," Melody said. "See you in the papers."

The door closed behind me. I took off at a sprint. I had to get to a pay phone. Quick. I had to tell somebody.

The first phone I found was in use. This guy in a basketball uniform was talking away. Everyone always says it's girls who gab, but I happen to know plenty of talkative boys. I loitered around for a while, but he started to glare at me. I dashed off to find another phone.

There was one outside the main office. I dropped in my quarter. The phone clicked and jingled. I punched in the number, which I knew by heart.

"Good evening, F. Scott's," said a polite voice. "May I help you?" It was Howie.

"This is Vickie Mahoney," I explained. "I'd like to talk to my dad, please. He's the cook there and—"

The voice answered with dignity. "I'll be happy to assist you in locating your father." He was laying on the maitre d' routine pretty thick.

"Great. I almost never call him at work, but I *have* to talk to him. It's an emergency."

"Oh! Don't move. I'll have him on the line in a flash."

He put me on hold, and a schmaltzy version of "Oh, What a Beautiful Morning" started playing. I sang along. Our school put on *Oklahoma!* last year, and I have all the songs memorized.

The line clicked. "Vickie? Vickie?" It was my father's panic-stricken voice. "What's wrong? What happened?"

"*Wrong?* Nothing's wrong, Dad."

"But Howie said it was an emergency."

"Well, not exactly an emergency."

His voice was heavy with irritation. "Victoria Hope Mahoney. I nearly had a heart attack. Never use the word 'emergency' unless it's a genuine, actual, bona fide emergency!" He paused. "Okay," he said, more calmly. "Why the call?"

Suddenly there was a thundering clatter of metal. The phone cracked against a hard surface. Then silence.

"Dad? Dad? What was that?"

He came back to the line. "An emergency. A *real* emergency. That's what one sounds like. The pot rack just fell. The whole day's been like this." He muffled the receiver. "Larry, I'll be there in one second. All right, Victoria, tell me. Why'd you call?"

"Today I was interviewed by a reporter from the *Keats Crier*. She asked me all kinds of crazy questions. I feel like a celebrity or something."

"Honey, that's terrific. You can tell me all about it tonight."

"But you won't get home until after my bedtime."

"Oh, right. At breakfast, then. Sorry I'm so rushed. It's nuts over here; you wouldn't believe it. We'll talk soon. All right?"

"See you, Dad."

I considered calling Mom next; then I decided against it. With my luck, I'd probably interrupt a counseling session with someone in deep, dark depression. Wrapping my scarf around my face, I headed outside.

The December wind blasted me, but I hardly felt it. There was a glow around me. Maybe this was how it felt to be a superstar. *Victoria*, I thought, *you sure are getting conceited*. Still, I couldn't wait to give someone all the details.

Matthew was standing in the Johnstons' front yard, kneedeep in snow.

"Howdy, Squirt," I called. "Who're you supposed to be? Frosty the Snowman?"

He came out to the gate. His small face was a puckered scowl.

"What's wrong with *you*?" I asked.

"Nothin'. I want to go home."

On our front steps, I twirled my key ring on one finger. "Watch this," I said. "Fastest key in the Midwest." A twist of my wrist, and the front door swung open. "Welcome to the Mahoney Mansion," I bellowed. I was feeling pretty good because finally I had someone to tell about the interview, even if it was only Matthew.

But he didn't budge. He plunked down on the front step with his elbows on his knees.

"I'm gonna wait for Mom," he said stubbornly.

"You can't sit out here. You'll freeze."

"Who cares?"

I sighed. Never try to argue with a six-year-old. That's my theory.

"Just don't come crying to me when you get frostbite and all your fingers fall off," I told him. I slammed the door. Then I opened it again. "Come inside when icicles start forming on your chin."

Not even a smirk.

Everyone was in a crummy mood. Some Christmas spirit. I shucked off my coat and went straight to the kitchen. The refrigerator was stocked. Rummaging, I found cut-up vegetables and homemade avocado dip. An after-school snack extraordinaire, as Dad would say. I polished off three carrots, one slice of celery, and half a green pepper.

The green bomb crunched into the driveway. I recognized the sound. I ran outside without a coat and yanked up the garage door. My brother was still sitting on the steps like a zombie.

"Here," I said, handing him a Kleenex. "Your nose is running." I wasn't sure, but I think he was crying.

"Mom, you'll never believe what happened to-day—" I shouted as she came up the walk. But she got one look at Matthew and turned her attention to him.

"Why are you sitting outside in this weather, my boy?"

She made us go inside and stomp the snow off our feet.

"Mom?" I said.

She waved me quiet. "First, Matthew. Tell me why you're upset."

My brother spoke in a rush. "I hate school. I'm never going back. If I don't go tomorrow, no one would miss me the next day, and I could skip the whole year. Okay?"

Mom unbuttoned her coat. "Not okay. Sorry."

My brother's eyes were soggy. He ground his fingers into his eye sockets, but the tears kept coming.

Mom looked tired. "Matthew, you have to go to school. It's a law. It's one of the drawbacks of being a kid."

Matthew slugged the back of the couch. He

kicked the upholstery. "They make fun of me."

"Mom, I have something to tell you about—" I began.

My mother turned, furiously. "Victoria, will you hush?"

I was stunned quiet. I stared at my feet. Their voices continued.

"Why do they make fun of you?" Mom asked my brother.

"They hate me."

"They don't hate you."

"Hate, hate, hate!"

"Honey, maybe you just need some help. Remember I told you we'd go talk to someone?"

"I don't want to talk to anyone!" Now he threw himself down on the cushions and screamed.

My feelings were throbbing with hurt. I backed into the kitchen.

From the living room, Mom's voice said: "When you're over this tantrum, Matthew, we'll talk again. Until then, I'll leave you alone."

The hall closet opened and closed. Then I heard her footsteps behind me. Cool as can be, I kept my back turned.

"I'm sorry I snapped at you," she said. "I'm so frustrated with your brother right now, and you were interrupting, and I just got angry."

I opened the refrigerator and fished out another carrot stick. I made my voice steely, as dignified as Howie the maitre d's. "*I* used to hate school, too.

But I never threw a fit like that."

"Matthew's problems are different than yours were," Mom said. "Come on. Battle over. What was it you wanted to tell me?"

I didn't feel like talking about the interview. For one thing, I didn't feel like a celebrity any more.

"Nothing," I said. "I'll help fix dinner."

10

Chelsie answered after the second ring.

"It's me," I said.

"I knew you were going to call," she said. "I've been sitting here by the phone waiting."

"Guess who got interviewed by a reporter from the *Keats Crier* today? I can't reveal her name, but she's a close personal friend of yours, and there will be a whole article about her in the next newspaper."

She gave a long, high squeal. I grinned, holding the phone away from my ear. I knew Chelsie would be excited, even if no one else was. "So that's why you couldn't walk home with me. I could have socked you for being so mysterious. Tell me all about it."

In slow, careful detail, I told her everything.

"It's too much," she said breathlessly. "Vic, you're going places."

I snickered. It was a pleasant thought.

Then she said, "Have you found a manager yet?"

"A *what?*"

"A manager. You know, someone to arrange your business affairs, set up your interviews, pick the outfits you'll wear on talk shows. That sort of thing."

"Chelsie," I said. "Aren't you going just a little bit overboard?"

Chels was just getting warmed up. "Nobody makes it to the top without a manager. The essay contest is small potatoes compared to what's ahead. So I hearby apply for the job. I'd make a great manager, Vic, because I have guts. I'm not afraid to call up total strangers and say, 'Hey, you really should talk to my client, Vickie Mahoney. She's got tons of talent.' "

It was true. Chelsie wasn't scared of anyone.

"Of course," she went on, "I'll need an expense account. In case I have to call TV producers in New York or California."

"Long distance calls are pretty expensive. Can you hold off on the long-distance calls until I get rich and famous?"

She sounded disappointed. "Okay. For now, I'll limit myself to local calls. By the way, when does the *Crier* article come out?"

"A couple of weeks."

"Look, I have to go. I've got ten zillion things to do. See you tomorrow."

The minute I hung up, the phone rang again. I lifted the receiver.

"Hello, hello," said a familiar, bubbling-happy voice. "Guess who's back in town?"

"Isadora!" I shouted.

"And me," said a second voice. "Your new Grandpa Wilkes."

"How was the honeymoon?" I asked. Then I blushed. Maybe it was impolite to ask about people's honeymoons.

But they didn't seem embarrassed. "More fun than a whole week at the state fair," Isadora told me. "The Guatemalan archaeological dig was a great idea."

I still thought it was an odd way to spend a honeymoon, but as I've said, Grandpa Wilkes and Isadora are not your typical couple.

"You should see our tans, Vickie." Isadora laughed into the phone. "The top of Harold's head is the color of a bing cherry."

They talked on and on, interrupting each other and guffawing. Finally I managed to slip in my news about winning second place in the contest.

There was a shocked silence on the other end of the line. Grandpa Wilkes was the first to speak.

"You just have to come and speak to the senior citizens' group," he said. "We've heard from politicians, heart doctors, aerobics teachers, and dog

59

trainers, but we've never met a real, live winner of a national writing contest."

I wiped my sweaty palms on my jeans. Even the thought made me nervous.

"I don't know," I said.

"Oh, come on. It's just a tiny group. Only seventy-five people or so."

I swallowed. *Seventy-five?* My heart gave a vicious little twist.

"Vickie, you still there? How about it? Let's make it for the end of this week. I'll arrange everything; I'll even stand up and make the introduction."

There was so much hope in his voice, I couldn't turn him down. I'm a sucker when it comes to grandparents. "I'll have to check with my manager," I said faintly.

"Manager?" Isadora sounded surprised.

"Chelsie. She's managing my appointments and stuff."

"Bring her, too," said Grandpa Wilkes in his hearty voice. "And invite your folks and that precious little brother of yours."

I was on the verge of telling them all the news about Matthew, too, but I changed my mind. It was too depressing. And now I had other things to worry about besides my brother. Like how in the world I was going to get through a speaking engagement at the senior citizens' center.

"My manager will be in touch," I said instead.

60

11

The scratchy Christmas records were playing, and the whole family was decorating the tree. All except Dad. He was on the couch, with his feet stretched to the coffee table. "Ah," he kept saying, exhaling. "This is the life."

"Sure." Mom hung another delicate piece of tinsel over a branch. "You lounge around, and we do all the work."

"I'm working," he said indignantly. "Haven't I been pointing out the bald spots? For instance, Bob, there's a branch to your immediate right that desperately needs an ornament. That's better."

I nibbled some peanut brittle. "It's okay, Dad," I chipped in. "This kind of work, I don't mind."

The tree was loaded. It glittered with the old familiar ornaments, even the ones Mom said were disgraceful. There was an angel with only one felt wing. (Matthew had eaten the other wing as a baby.) There were spotty gold bulbs. And there was an aluminum-foil star that I had made in kindergarten.

"Matthew," Dad called from his comfortable seat. "Put something in that empty spot to your left."

My brother started to hang a fuzzy mouse ornament.

"Left! *Left!*" said Dad.

"I don't know which is left," my brother muttered.

"Sure you do. We learned it months ago—" Dad began. I saw Mom flash him a look. He stopped.

Mom showed Matthew where to put the mouse. Then she announced, "Done."

We all stood back and looked.

"It's the most beautiful tree I ever saw," my brother said softly.

12

On Friday, two things happened.

Number one, my brother went to his first appointment with the learning disabilities specialist's.

Dad was driving. He had offered to drop Chels and me off at school, so the three of us were crunched up front. Matthew was in the rear. He was pretty quiet back there. Too quiet. We all peered at each other.

"You okay?" Dad said, finally. He made his voice real cheerful, like ho-ho-ho and jolly old Saint Nick and all of that, but it came off sort of forced.

"I'm okay," Matthew said after a second—but he sounded like his best friend had just moved to Timbuktu.

"For pete's sake," I said, twisting around. "Cheer

63

up. You look like you're going to the guillotine."

"What's a guillotine?"

On second thought, I decided it wouldn't be a good idea to talk about gory stuff like guillotines. "I'll tell you later—when you're older."

He sighed. "Rats."

I turned around. Part of me wanted to say, "Quit being such a baby." The other part wanted to say, "Boy, it's really crummy the way everyone keeps shuffling you around to see doctors and specialists. I'd hate it." It was a strange feeling.

Dad dropped us off at Keats. Chels and I climbed out.

"Good luck," I said to my brother. "Don't be nervous."

"So long," he answered with a lost-puppy look out of the window.

I slammed the door, and they drove away.

The second important thing that happened was my talk to Grandpa Wilkes' group of senior citizens that evening.

"Cheer up," Dad told me, as we stood at the back of the meeting room waiting for the program to start. "You look like you're going to the guillotine."

"Very funny."

There were elderly people mingling about. Some were munching on cookies. I had munched a few myself. Being nervous always makes me hungry.

"After all," Dad continued. "Your brother made

it through his scary event. I'm sure you'll survive, too."

"I was so nervous, I forgot to ask. How did his tests go? Did he pass?"

Dad chuckled, showing nice white teeth. He was a pleasant-looking man, I suddenly realized, in a dad-like, adult sort-of-way. I could see why Mom had fallen for him. "Vickie, you don't pass or fail diagnostic tests."

"Okay. How'd he do, all-in-all?"

"It will be a while before we have complete results, but Ms. Mulholland said there's definitely something wrong."

I try to be good in sensitive situations. I put my hand on his arm comfortingly. "I'm sorry, Dad," I said dramatically. "This must be a blow."

"Actually, I'm relieved. Ms. Mulholland was very encouraging. Now that we know something's wrong, maybe we can help Matthew."

My mom and Chelsie appeared, coffee in hand.

"Terry," Mom said. "We just met the most charming couple."

"It was so romantic," Chels said. "First we met the husband because he said I had pretty eyes. Then he went and got his wife. Her name is Olga. She's beautiful. He said that he came over on a boat from Russia back around 1917 or something and worked and saved for *two years* before he could afford to send for her. Finally, between the two of them, they had enough for a boat fare. He had to wait for months, of course, but finally the boat was due to arrive and he went out to the port. He told us what it was like when he first saw her coming toward him at the pier—with 'eyes like velvet' —that's what he said. 'Eyes like a quiet Russian night.' "

Chels blew on her coffee. "If some guy ever said that to me I'd probably keel over in shock. I like old people. They're . . . more refined."

"I just hope they're too refined to go to sleep when they have to listen to boring speakers," I said.

Grandpa Wilkes got everyone settled down.

"And now," he said in a booming voice, "it's with great pride that I introduce to you my talented and award-winning granddaughter."

The room clattered with applause while I went up front. When it was quiet again, I leaned toward the mike. "I wrote this essay about individuality," I said, and my voice sounded squeaky. "I guess I'll go ahead and read it to you."

"That would be nice," a woman in the front row said. She had a pretty, wrinkly-pink face.

A gentleman sitting kitty-corner nodded approvingly.

And Isadora called, "Go to it, baby!"

I cleared my throat and began.

At the end, there was a short silent pause. Then the clapping started. They clapped and clapped. Isadora and Grandpa Wilkes gave me a standing ovation, but of course that didn't count. Not really.

Everyone knows grandparents are biased.

Stiffly, I walked down the aisle. Probably I looked like a wooden soldier. The faintest little smile was struggling to come to my lips.

At the back of the room Dad passed me a sly look. "Don't let this go to your head," he hissed. But he had a hard time hiding his grin, too.

13

I jerked my head up sharply.

Outside my bedroom door, I had heard a creak on the stairs. It was a familiar noise, just like the sound knees make when they crack.

But it was impossible. Mom and Dad were at a Saturday night church party, and Matthew was sawing logs. It was just me and my homework—and Bullrush, of course. The two of us were sprawled on my bed. We listened tensely for a second or two. Then I whispered to Bullrush: "You're imagining things again."

I went back to my history book.

Studying on weekends is not one of life's greatest pleasures. Especially if you happen to know that just a few miles away your friends are having an overnight party without you.

Kristie had invited me, of course, but I had already promised I'd baby-sit Matthew. Just thinking about it made my head hurt, so I tried not to. I was also a tiny bit angry at my brother. I tried not to think about that, either.

The stairway creaked again.

Now I was really scared. I pulled the blanket over my head and waited, shivering. The stranger was advancing up the stairs, inch by inch, step by step. . . .

"Surprise!" shouted a voice.

"Matthew, you rat!" I threw off the covers. He was laughing his head off. His mouth was open wide, showing the rows of white baby teeth.

"You're not mad at me, are you?" he asked, stopping suddenly.

"Yes, I'm mad at you." I swung one leg off the bed, then the other. "You're supposed to be asleep. And you shouldn't sneak up on people! Now go to bed!"

He plunked down on the end of my bed and squashed his face into Bullrush's side. "I don't feel like it."

"I don't care." I started to drag him by his pajama top. He slid on the floor in his bare feet.

"Vickie, I want to stay here with you. I can't sleep."

I let go, and he lurched toward the bed again.

"Listen," I told him. "I have tons of homework to do. Absolutely tons, understand? Maybe if you did homework, you wouldn't have so much trouble in school."

I guess I'd been thinking that for a while, but I was as surprised as Matthew was when it came blurting out.

His arms hung straight at his sides.

"There's something wrong with me," he said. "That's what Mr. Crawford says. I'm dumb."

Now I jumped in with, "You're not *dumb*, Matthew." At least that's what everyone was telling *me*. I wasn't so sure anymore.

"No one wants to be my friend at school 'cause I'm so dumb. I can't learn anything."

Downstairs, the phone rang.

"Go back to bed!" I said to Matthew. "Now!"

I ran down the three flights of stairs and pounced on the phone. "Hello?" I said, panting into the receiver.

"It's me." Chelsie sounded like she was out of breath, too. "I had to call." There were high-pitched screams and laughter in the background, and Chels had to shout above them. "We just played this crazy game. Guess who was 'It'?"

"You."

"Bingo. I had to put on red long underwear over my clothes, and everyone stuffed me with balloons, and at the signal they all chased me around and popped the balloons with pins. It was crazy!"

There was a loud pop and a shriek. Chels giggled. "Did I break your eardrum?" she asked. "Peggy just got the last one."

"Sounds like a riot and a half," I told her, wrapping myself tightly in the phone cord.

"Now we're going to eat these fancy cookies her mom made and watch *It's a Wonderful Life* on TV. You know which one I'm talking about? It's the Christmas movie with Jimmy Stewart in it."

"I know which one. It's a good thing I'm not there. I always cry my eyes out at the end."

"I wish you were here. I wouldn't care if you cried buckets of tears."

It was hard to talk. "Me, too," I managed. I felt sick.

"What are *you* doing, Vic?"

"Nothing much," I said. "Just keeping an eye on my little brother. After we hang up I'm going to turn on *It's a Wonderful Life* and cry myself silly."

A sudden noise on the stairs made me jump. I peeked around the door. Matthew was sneaking down the stairs. He had a wicked smile on his face.

"I have to go now," I said.

Chelsie said, "Okay, but this is probably my last call tonight. I'll see you in church tomorrow morning, okay?"

"Over and out." I hung up.

I closed my eyes. Automatically, I launched into one of my on-the-spot prayers. "Dear Lord, teach me patience—now." I stopped. Then I went ahead and added exactly what I was thinking. You might as well be honest with God; He knows everything anyway. "Because there's no telling what I'll do to my brother when I get ahold of him."

I breathed deeply three times. Then I opened my eyes.

14

I raced down the hall, with Peggy Hiltshire right behind me. Another minute and I'd be late for class. I was going a hundred miles an hour.

"Slow up," Peg's poor pathetic voice called behind me. "Vick-ie. Hey! Vickie Mahoney, you stop right now and talk to me."

I squealed to a stop. "Peg, I'm almost late. You don't want me to be late, do you? Just try to keep up."

She picked up the pace again. Lockers whizzed by, and kids with armloads of books looked like dazed statues standing still.

Peg shouted over the pounding of our shoes. "I want to say 'I'm sorry' about what I said to you guys the other day. You know. At lunch."

"Huh?" I was thinking about my assignment. Had I left it in my locker after all? "Peggy, that was over a week ago."

"I know, but it was stupid what I said about being popular and stuff. I didn't mean that you guys *weren't* popular, I meant that Jennifer and Susie are so popular they can hardly see straight. But you should meet them, they're not so bad. Oh, I'm messing this up royally."

We pulled up outside my room, gasping. If you want to know the truth, I am not in that great shape.

"I . . . understand . . . what you mean," I said.

"You do understand?" Her voice skimmed the ceiling, along with her eyebrows. "I'm so re-*lieved*. I thought you-all hated me. Want to be friends again?"

I smiled. When I first met her, I thought Peggy was stuck up. But things change. People change. Even I had changed. And Peggy had a way of growing on you.

"I'm glad you're not mad," she said. "Now you can autograph my *Crier*. I just got my copy."

She yanked a folded-up paper out of her notebook. "Your article's on the back. See? Right by the piece about the orchestra's special Christmas program."

I peered at the typed pages. I tried to make sense of the articles, but the letters seemed to be jumping.

74

"Here, silly," Peg said, pulling the paper away from me. "Look. 'Keats Sophomore Hits Big Time!' "

Finally I found the article. The headline was in big black type. Beneath it, in smaller type, the subheadline read: "Vickie Mahoonie wins the big bucks in national contest."

"*Mahoonie?*" I said. "*Vickie Mahoonie?*"

"Close enough," she said, shrugging.

The bell rang. Peg grabbed her paper back. "Autograph—after class," she yelled to me as she slid into the room next door.

Blushing, I walked the three rows to my seat. As I passed by, a kid I hardly knew pointed to the article. "Good job, ace," he said. I blushed deeper and slid into my place.

15

When Dad is home for the evening, it's great.

Sometimes on his nights off, he and Mom work around the house. This is boring. They are serious fix-ups and always messing around with screwdrivers and 3/8" power drill bits. (I only know about this stuff because in my house someone is always yelling for me to "Hand over that monkey wrench" or something.) Our place needs plenty of sprucing up.

But some nights we're lazy. Mom gets a cracking orange fire going in the fireplace. I make popcorn. And we just sit around. Tonight was one of those nights.

The room had a nice, warm Christmas mood.

Dad put a record on. Lying on the floor, I smiled to myself. I had a secret. Big news. But I was savoring it, like candy. I had already tried to imagine their faces when I told them, but I couldn't.

"One of these days," Dad was saying, "We need to plan our Christmas-vacation-cross-country-ski-ing-trip. But not tonight. I'm too comfy."

"Amen." Mom kicked off her shoes and stretched her legs. "Right now I don't want to do anything but just sit here and—"

Just then my brother came roaring into the room, flying his balsa-wood airplane.

"No running in the house," Mom said.

He clutched the plane in his little fingers. The airplane did loop-de-loops. It swooped and whirled. It went into a nose dive toward the carpet.

"Matthew!" said Dad sharply.

The plane crashed—with sound effects.

Dad's voice was very calm. "Didn't you hear me?"

Matthew looked confused. "I don't know."

"Well, now you do. You can play quietly, can't you?"

He shrugged.

"Try."

Matthew's airplane made a smooth takeoff and headed for the western light—an old coffee table lamp.

The cat settled back down to his snooze. Maybe now was the time to tell them the news. I rehearsed the words. Now that I had waited so long, I wanted to get it right.

"Mom, Dad—"

Mom jumped up with a cry as Matthew ran into the lamp going full speed. The light crashed to the floor. I was blinded by a sudden flash of anger, even though I knew it had been an accident. I was tired of accidents.

Mom breathed in once. Then she said, "It's okay. Nothing's broken. Just be more careful." She placed the lamp back on the end table.

A few quiet seconds passed. My nerves were shot. *Cut it out*, I told myself. *It's not* that *big of a deal*.

"I had an interesting offer today," I said, at last. (Yes, that was cool.) "From channel 4 television. They're sending an interviewer to school tomorrow. With cameras and everything. Ms. Runebach-Dahl arranged it. I'll be on the news."

Mom and Dad stared at me as if they'd been punched.

"Say something," I said.

Mom shook her head as if to clear cobwebs. "I can't believe it," she said. "No one in the Mahoney family has ever been on television."

"Are you nervous?" Dad asked.

"Not yet. I've had practice in public speaking, you know, at the senior citizens' center."

"That's true," he agreed, nodding his head seriously. "You're becoming an old pro."

Suddenly Matthew came stumbling into me, kicking me hard in the side. "You were in my way!" he shouted as he fell.

"You did that on purpose," I said.

"I did not!" His face was red, and tears were already brimming up in his brown eyes.

"Oh, don't bawl," I said.

"You can't tell me what to do!"

Dad spoke in that strange, calm voice. "What we don't need," he said, "is another spell. Everyone cool down."

"She tripped me!" Matthew's mouth was open, and his voice was a yell.

"Oh, Matt," Mom said.

Dad retrieved the mashed airplane. "Time out. Let's go upstairs and get ready for bed."

"No. I don't want to! How come Vickie gets to stay up? She's the favorite!"

"Let's go, partner." When Matthew sat down on the carpeting and refused to budge, Dad scooped him up. As they passed by, they did not have happy faces.

Mom and I listened to the footsteps going up the stairs.

"Well," Mom said with a sigh. "Dinner dishes don't get done by themselves. Feel like helping me?"

I stood up, rubbing my sore ribs. "Might as well."

She washed, I dried. I rubbed every plate hard with the towel; I was in that kind of mood.

Mom wasn't acting normal. Usually she talks up a storm while we do dishes.

"You okay?" I asked her shyly.

"I'm depressed. Parents get depressed, too, you know." She handed me a soapy plate. I rinsed and dried it and stacked it in the cupboard.

"I talked to the specialist again today," she continued. "We know for certain that Matthew has a learning disability. The specialist says it's genetic, but I can't help feeling that if I'd been a better mother, if we'd noticed earlier—"

"It's not your fault," I said. It worried me that her face was lined and sad. Sometimes you don't think about parents having feelings. But when you *do* realize it, it can make you feel pretty terrible. "I think you're a superb mother."

That made her smile a little. "Thanks, Vickie. I guess it will take a while before I believe that, but thanks."

She took a brave breath and straightened up. "We're going to set up regular meetings with the specialist. She'll work with Matthew and teach us new ways to help him learn. The goal is to help him be more organized, pay attention, and remember the stuff he needs to learn."

I just let her talk.

"If it weren't for—" she stopped, as if she had said too much. "Well, I may as well let the cat out of the bag. There's another reason I'm feeling low. Your father and I had finally gotten the courage to think about adding another little Mahoney to the family. Now it looks like we'll have to put it off. We were

80

looking forward to having a baby."

I absorbed this information, drying Tupperware slowly. "A baby?"

"A baby."

I smiled. Ever since our baby Jessica died, I had wondered if they would have another. It would be fun to have a sweet little powdery baby around the house.

"—But with Matthew going through this . . . I don't know. He probably couldn't handle the stress. And I don't know if *I* could, either."

The dry taste of disappointment came to my mouth. Matthew and his dumb problems.

"Don't blame your brother," Mom said fiercely, as if she had read my mind. "None of this is his fault. He's doing his best."

I didn't have more to say. We stood side by side, washing and drying in rhythm.

I climbed up to my bedroom early that night. I wanted to make some notes about the book I was going to write. I got out my lucky writer's pen and began:

Story—family that had nothing but problems. The mom and dad are noble, but poor. So poor that they can't afford to buy their teenaged daughter beautiful clothes. Because of this, her budding career as a TV star is ruined. Plus they have a grouchy son who is a slow learner and into everything, and he keeps breaking the few pieces of furniture they do *have. Every day, a new disaster.*

But how would I end it? That was the hard part. Leaning on my elbows, I thought hard. Nothing came into my head. I hung my head over the side of the bed. (Getting the old blood up to the brain.) Zip.

Then I stopped. The Bible had a story about a guy with problems. Old Job *really* had it tough. Maybe if I checked how he got through his problems, I'd get some inspiration for my book. I'd keep my story ultra-modern, so no one could accuse me of copying. I could always throw in a couple of VCRs and some space travel.

I whipped out my Bible and paged to the story. (I'm a whiz with a Bible; I always win Bible drills.)

The stuff that happened to Job was even worse than I remembered. His kids died. His animals and his servants were taken away. Pretty devastating stuff. He only got through it by trusting God.

"But there's no one as perfect as Job," I muttered. "How are normal people supposed to survive this stuff?" I know God hears silent prayers, but sometimes I like talking out loud to Him. It makes Him seem closer.

I read a few verses again. On second thought, Job sounded like an ordinary guy. It wasn't like he wasn't *tempted* to get angry and upset and blame God for his problems. But he went on trusting.

I stared out my window. The world looked like

the inside of a freezer. White. And cold. And lonely.

"It's not that easy to trust You," I said, above the howling of the wind outside. "I've been on some pretty rough rides lately."

Then I put down my pen and got down beside the bed. "If You'll help me, I'll do my best to trust you, God," I said. "Really."

16

"The light bothering you?"

The channel 4 news reporter leaned down and gave me his flashy white smile. Squinting through the glare of TV video light, I shook my head. I don't think I could have gotten words out of my dry mouth. The light was fine; actually, his teeth were more dazzling.

"Hold on, Vickie," he said. "We'll get rolling in just a second here." He turned to Ms. Runebach-Dahl, and they talked together in low tones.

Kids stood around the classroom peering at me. It was pretty nerve-wracking. No one likes to be stared at. I clutched a sweaty copy of my essay.

Suddenly the reporter roared: "Okay, roll 'em!"

Everyone jumped. Me especially. "Just a little TV-style humor," he explained.

Ms. Runebach-Dahl came and stood by me. The lights went on again. Mr. Reporter took his position in front of us, and the interview began.

"I'm visiting Keats Junior High School to talk with a budding young artist," he said in his reporter-voice. He was really good. I bet he had to go to school to learn to talk that way. "An eighth-grade student by the name of Victoria Mahoney is winner of second place in the annual Scholastic Writing Contest. That's quite an honor for a barely-thirteen-year-old." He swiveled in my direction. The glaring eye of the camera followed. "How do you feel about winning a national contest, Vickie?" he asked, sticking the microphone in my face.

"It's really nice," I said. "I like it." Inside I curled into a microscopic ball. *Dumb! That was so dumb!*

"What topic did you choose for your award-winning essay?"

"It was about individuality."

"Can you describe what that means?"

"I guess that it's important to be yourself and not worry about being weird if you have to be."

He smiled. "Are you an individual, Vickie?"

"I try. It's not so easy."

His face seemed empty. I couldn't tell if I was doing okay or not. "And here is the teacher behind the award. Grace Runebach-Dahl nominated Victoria to write in the contest. Why did you choose Vickie to represent the school, Ms. Runebach-Dahl?"

Ms. Runebach-Dahl was very cool; she smiled and spoke clearly. "Vickie is the sort of student one meets only once in a while. She's a talented writer as well as an excellent pupil. In a word—or two—I'd say she's unusually creative."

The reporter looked at me. "Do you agree with that, Vickie?"

I laughed. "I guess so."

"How were you rewarded for your efforts?"

"A check for $125," I told him, not quite able to keep back the grin. "Actually I haven't gotten it yet, but . . ."

The kids in the classroom sighed in admiration. Or maybe it was envy. It was hard to tell which.

"Go ahead and read a few lines from your work."

The pages shook, but I went ahead. In a strong, brave voice I read the first paragraph of my essay. I got better near the end.

"That's fine," he said, signaling to me.

Next they taped the sign-off segment. The reporter stood near the bulletin board that said "Books Are Our Friends." He cleared his throat.

"An inspired creation by an inspiring girl," he said, letting the big smile shine again. "For WCOO television, this is Julian Chandler in Minneapolis." He waved to the camera man. The light went off and the man lowered the camera.

While the other guy was gathering up equipment, Julian shook Ms. Runebach-Dahl's hand. Then he came over and shook mine, too. "Watch yourself on the five o-clock report tomorrow night, sweetheart," he said.

Chels, who had been standing in the back of the room, approached, smirking. "As your manager, may I say that you did great?"

"Go ahead."

"You did great."

"Thank you. Want to come over tomorrow night and watch me be great all over again?"

"I wouldn't miss it. Hey, let's invite some people. Do you think your parents would mind? It would be very good for exposure."

"They won't mind. Invite away."

The bell shrieked, and everyone started piling out into the hallway.

"Gotta go," Chels said. Glancing over her shoulder she grinned evilly and said, "See you later —sweetheart."

17

Chels walked me home, talking a mile a minute.

"—And about tomorrow night. I invited Kristie, Janell, and Peggy. Do you have any other contacts?"

I didn't even know what a contact was.

"You don't?" Chels said. "Luckily you have a manager who can keep you informed of important terms like that. A contact is someone who can help advance your career."

"Peg, Kristie, and Janell can advance my career?"

"Well, I have to fudge a little. You're too new in the business to have many contacts with media people."

"Yeah, I can't even think of *one*."

"Never mind. Leave everything to me. Think of

this as a dry run for the real thing, someday. I have big plans for you, kid, big plans."

We stopped outside my house. Our breath made frozen puffs in the air. In a little while the afternoon would slip away in a tangerine-colored sunset, and cold night would fade in.

Suddenly Chels leaned over the fence. "Hi, Matthew," she said.

My brother was making snow angels in the front yard. Very small angels.

"In case you've forgotten," I said grouchily, you're supposed to be at the Johnstons'. You're supposed to wait there until I pick you up."

"Not today." He flapped his arms and legs. "Today Mom and I went to the learning specialist. She came home early to take me."

Chels looked at me. I looked at Chels. It was weird to hear such a little kid use a term like "learning specialist."

Chels said she had to take off, so I went inside, slamming the door.

"Don't slam," came my mother's voice.

"Sorry."

Even from the living room I could smell hot cocoa. I have a thing about cocoa. I pulled off my coat and mittens and stuffed them in the closet.

"You're not supposed to be here until after five," I called.

Mom, Isadora, and Grandpa Wilkes were all sitting around the kitchen table. Papers and booklets

89

cluttered the table top. They each had a steaming mug.

Mom spoke up. "Didn't I tell you? From now on, I take Matthew to the specialist every Wednesday afternoon."

"Oh," I said, "That explains why *you're* here." I poured myself a brim-full cup of cocoa and pulled up a chair. "What are *you* guys doing here?" I asked.

Isadora slapped her hand on the table. "How do you like that? Talk about a warm welcome."

I smiled sheepishly. "You know what I mean."

"To answer your question, Vickie, your mother invited us."

"I came because I smelled cocoa," Grandpa said, wiggling his eyebrows at me like Groucho Marx.

"Look at all this stuff." Mom gestured with a wave of her hand. "It's all about learning disabilities."

"Great," I said. "Everything I ever wanted to know—and more."

Mom looked at me, and her eyes were bright and eager. "You should read some of this stuff. *Lots* of kids have learning problems. And we can actually do things to help Matthew."

"Like what?"

"Get him on a routine, for one thing. You know how disorganized he's been? He needs a schedule. Some LD kids can't keep information straight in their memory. It's too much to remember—get dressed, wash up, eat breakfast, brush teeth. If we set a routine for him to follow, he might feel less confused in the mornings.

"And maybe you could help him study, sometimes," she continued. Her face was so hopeful, I couldn't quite look at her. The last thing I wanted to do was study with my little brother.

"—He'll learn at a different pace than other kids," she went on, "and it will probably be harder for him to memorize information. But even if he isn't the whiz kid of his class, he can still learn. He'll even get better at his social skills. You know, hobnobbing with other humans. Matthew used to have loads of friends."

Isadora drained her cup. "I'll help him find other activities that he enjoys," she said, "so he'll feel successful in something. Maybe I'll get him painting. All Shippleys have a creative streak."

"And he can help me at the senior citizens' center," said Mr. Wilkes. "I could use an assistant with my craft lessons."

"I warn you," Mom said, her lips curling. "He can be a handful."

"That's the truth," I said.

18

"Hand over that popcorn!" I shouted at Janell.
"—Please," I added, as Mom came into the family
room. Parents like you to have good manners even
when you're just talking to your friends.

Janell, Chels, Peg, Kristie, and I were all mashed
onto the couch. It was a tight fit. We had the TV
turned low, waiting for the big moment when I
would appear on the screen. In the meantime, we
were snacking—"stuffing our faces," as Chelsie
would say. Kristie had brought leftover cookies from
her overnight party. I reached for another.

"No fair!" Chels screeched, slapping my hand.
"You've eaten all the ones with chocolate stars. That
last one is mine."

"Mine!" Kristie shouted, making a dive for it.

"Mine!" Peg leaned forward suddenly and snatched it off the plate. Before any of us could move, she had taken a bite.

"You little snitch!" Quick as a flash, Chels pulled a hunk of cookie from between Peg's teeth and popped it into her own mouth.

We went crazy. I fell forward on the floor. Janell fell on top of me. The muffled snorts of Kristie and Peg continued on the couch above us.

Mom spoke. "What a dignified group of young ladies."

Still snickering, we pulled ourselves together. Just as we got comfortable again, the theme music for channel 4 news started.

"Turn it up, turn it up!" Kristie shouted.

I twisted the volume button.

"Matthew," Mom called. "Come on! Your sister's going to be on television!" She pulled up a seat.

The camera focused on the serious-faced news anchors. They talked about fires and burglaries and the latest drug busts. We all just sat there, glued to the set. The longer they talked, the more tense I got.

"How come I'm so nervous?" I whispered to Chelsie. "I already did the interview. What have I got to be nervous about?"

"Nervousness is human nature," she said wisely, as if she were Sigmund Freud or someone. "Relax. You need to get used to stuff like this. It's just a matter of time before the West Coast calls to ask you to do a talk show or two. Johnny Carson, of course, puts writers on last, after the singers and actors and comedians. But publicity is publicity."

"Ssshh!" said Kristie, leaning forward.

Dave, the anchor man, was smiling and talking about today's amazing young people, and suddenly Julian Chandler appeared on the screen, clutching his microphone.

"It's him," I whispered.

Kristie let out a sigh. "He's gorgeous."

"Do you think his teeth are real?" Mom wanted to know. "I've heard of pearly-whites, but those are ridiculous."

Before I could answer, Peg suddenly screamed. She was pointing to the TV screen.

"There you are!" said Janell, pointing, too.

It was me, all right, bigger than life. I looked scared.

"You look great!" Kristie said. "A little scared, but—"

"Quiet, everybody," said Mom. "Listen."

Julian talked and I talked, and I sat there thinking maybe I didn't sound so dumb, after all. Even the "It's nice" comment didn't make me seem like a complete idiot.

Chelsie looked at me proudly, like a manager. "You're a natural, Vic, old buddy."

About then my brother came tromping in. He sat down right in front of the tube.

"Hey!" everyone yelled. "Move!"

94

He finally got his body out of the line of vision, but he was really acting like a smart-aleck. Mom shot me a look.

In just a couple of minutes the interview was over. We all sighed and sat back.

"Boy," said Matthew. "That was boring. You sure said some dumb things."

Probably if my friends hadn't all been there, I would have clobbered him. The anchor man was saying nice stuff about me—calling kids like me "gifted" and "Minnesota's most precious natural resource," and I just sat there with my arms folded, wanting to bash my stupid brother.

Then I remembered how I had promised God I would trust Him. Probably God wouldn't approve of me bashing Matthew. So I just smiled at the television anchor and said, "Thanks. Thanks, loads."

My friends giggled. They appreciate good sarcasm.

"You were just kidding, weren't you, Matthew?" Mom prompted him. "Just making a joke?"

Matthew looked around. All eyes were on him. Finally he nodded. "Yeah. I was kidding."

"That was a good one," said Chels, nudging him. She's good with Matthew. Sometimes she has more patience than I do.

Mom noticed all the sugary snacks on the coffee table and made a face. "Wait here," she ordered. In a second she returned from the kitchen carting a gigantic tray, loaded with vegetables. Everyone reached in for cucumbers and stuff.

Of course my brother hung around acting silly. He had never seemed odd before, but now everything he did reminded me that he wasn't like every other kid. I just hoped no one would notice and think he was retarded or something. The old logic tried to kick in: "He's just acting like a normal kid," I told myself. But I was still tense.

Then Peg said she'd "just absolutely love" to see Matthew's balsa wood airplane, and he charged out of the room to get it.

"I've said it before, Vickie," Peggy said to me. "Your brother is the cutest."

"I wish my brother was cute," said Kristie, sighing. "He's just gross. He's a slob. You should see how messy he leaves the bathroom sometimes. Towels everywhere, toothpaste in the sink. Bleck."

I was thinking something that I couldn't say out loud. "If only Matthew were normal like other kids," was the thought racing around in my head, "I wouldn't care if he *was* a slob."

And I was still thinking it when he came tearing back into the room with his old bashed-up airplane.

19

Usually Saturday is a work day. The house fills with the racket of hammering and sawing, and—above it all—the sound of Dad whistling cheerfully.

But this day I couldn't find Mom and Dad in any of the usual work spots. I hunted all over. The house was quiet.

Finally I found them. Mom was wrapped in her peach robe, and her feet were in fuzzy rabbit slippers. Dad had on his grey sweats. They both looked up from their books when I came into their bedroom.

"Hi," they mumbled together and went back to reading.

I flopped down on the end of the bed. "How

come you're in your lazy clothes?" I asked after a second.

"Isn't it obvious?" said Mom. "We're being low-energy, no-good, do-nothing slobs."

"And," Dad added, grinning, "we're loving every second of it."

"But," I pointed out, "it's four o'clock in the afternoon on a Saturday. You could be stripping woodwork or fooling around with the plumbing. Don't you feel guilty?"

Mom considered this seriously. Then she shrugged. "Nope. We need a break. We've been under a lot of stress lately."

"Yeah," said Dad. "Don't remind us of loose floorboards and unpainted walls. This carefree attitude could vanish in an instant."

You can't always reason with parents. That's one thing I've learned. So I didn't try. I just stayed around; I hung my head over the end of the bed for a while. All the blood raced to my head. Maybe I'd stay like this forever. Maybe I'd never move from this spot, until I turned into a fossil and they had to cart me away to the Smithsonian and put me in a plexiglass exhibit case.

Mom gave me a poke with the toe of one slipper. "Something wrong?"

"Mmmpp," I said.

"What was that?"

"Nothing."

The room was silent again. I exhaled softly.

The room was still silent. I sighed louder.

Dad sat up. "All right. You've been moping around here like Juliet Capulet. What's wrong?"

"It's Matthew." That surprised even me. I hadn't meant to blurt it out that way.

"Something's wrong with Matthew?" Mom asked innocently, her eyes round.

"Oh, Mom," I said impatiently, sitting up fast and nearly giving myself whiplash. "You know something's wrong with him. He's not normal. He's got big problems!"

The room suddenly felt as big and empty as a mountain cave. I could almost hear my voice echoing: "Big problems! Big problems!" Maybe Mom and Dad could too, because they didn't move. They just stared at me as if they'd been zapped with stun guns.

"So?" Dad said. "Everyone's got problems." His voice had just a dash of anger in it. "Problems are normal. He wouldn't be human if he didn't have problems."

"That's not what I mean!" I said. "I'm talking about his . . . disability." Warm tears crowded up behind my eyeballs. I swallowed. I smoothed the bedspread, even though it didn't need smoothing. If there's one thing I hate it's starting to cry when you're trying to make a serious point. "He's nothing but trouble lately, and even when he's naughty he doesn't get into trouble and he never works on school work and I'm sick of having him around!"

There was a lot I *wasn't* saying. Like "We've had enough problems!" and "We've lost Jessica, and now we have a dopey kid who can't learn to read?" and "How come we never have any money, like other people?" But I didn't feel like going into all of that.

Mom closed her book quietly. I thought she would be angry, but instead she smiled. She leaned over and patted my hand. "I have an idea," she said, in a peaceful voice. "Come with me to the clinic on Wednesday. You can tell the learning-disability specialist all of that. Maybe she'll have some ideas. I'll call Monday and set up the appointment."

I closed my mouth, which had fallen open.

"Me?" I said. "Why me? I'm not the one with the disability."

Dad flipped his book shut, too. *Crack!* "This is a family matter. You're involved whether you like it or not. I think your mother's suggestion is dandy. I'll come, too."

"Great. Let me just put it down in my calendar so I don't forget—"

I tried to get a word in, but they were already talking about times and who would pick up whom. I talked louder. "I don't see why *I* have to go. I'm just the sister."

"Don't be nervous." Dad patted my arm, just the way Mom had, as if I were a nervous Cocker Spaniel. "We'll just talk."

I stood up. "I guess I'll be leaving," I said with as much dignity as I could stuff into one sentence, "since my opinion doesn't seem to matter."

"Okay," said Dad, smiling.

"Okay," said Mom, smiling.

"If anyone wants me, I'll be in my room."

I waited for them to stop me, but they were both picking up their books again.

I turned and marched out with my head held up high.

20

"Want to hear an interesting fact about eye shadow?" Chelsie asked. She was peering into my makeup mirror, making an incredible face. With her mouth open and her eyes half-shut, she looked just like a monster I once saw in a Saturday matinee movie. I decided not to tell her this.

"Yeah," I said. "Tell me something interesting about eye shadow."

"It's impossible to get on straight. Have you ever noticed? No matter how many of those Merry Makeup demonstrations I go to, I can never get both lids on evenly." She straightened up. "Hey. Aren't you ready yet? We're going to be late for school. Not to mention the fact that I'm roasting in this coat."

"I think I'll wear thish." My voice came out garbled; I had my head half-jammed through the neck of a pale blue turtleneck. I jumped into my black jeans and slipped socks over my feet. Ready. It took a second to approve myself in the mirror. I frowned. Yes, I looked conservative enough. Today was the day I'd meet the learning specialist. "So you're Matthew Mahoney's big zeester," I imagined her saying, as she looked me over with slitty rat eyes. "Let's zee how intelligent *ve* are." I wanted to look as normal as possible.

"Victoria, get a move on!" Matthew's voice carried all the way up the stairs to my bedroom. He sounded just like Mom.

I tried to yell back: "I'm almost ready, all right, already!" but it's hard to sound sarcastic when you're shouting.

Chels and I pounded down two flights.

Mom and Matthew were standing at the bottom of the stairs with their arms crossed.

"Hmm," said Mom, looking at her watch.

Matthew rolled his eyes. "Jeepers, what a slowpoke."

Chelsie just went to the closet, grabbed my coat, and held it up. I shoved one arm through a sleeve and gave Mom the fastest hug of a lifetime. "You're picking me up tonight?"

"Right after school. Don't be late!"

I danced outside to the sidewalk, waving. "Who do you think I am? Matthew?"

"Hey," said my brother, following us outside.

For once the day roared by; Christmastime makes life move fast. Caroling choir members roved the halls, and for lunch there were little squares of white cake with red and green frosting. I have noticed that everyone seems friendlier on the last week before Christmas vacation. Even gym teachers.

The end of the school day came quickly, and before I knew it I was looking out for Mom's car. Chelsie waited with me in the main hallway.

"You nervous?" she asked, after a long silence. Only the sounds of the orchestra practicing for their big Christmas concert interrupted the after-school quiet.

I shrugged, trying to look calm. "A little. What if she starts asking me questions? 'How do you feel about your brother? Do you love him the way a good sister should?' I'll probably have to tell her the truth—that I think he's been pretty creepy lately."

"Boy," said Chels, sighing. "Compared to yours right now, my life is tame." She sounded jealous.

"There's Mom," I said, tearing through the door. "So long."

Right on time we picked up Dad.

"Hello, my beauties," he said, wedging himself into the seat with us. He leaned over to kiss Mom, and for a minute I felt like I'd been thrown into the middle of a movie love scene. I guess it's a good sign when your parents are still mushy.

"The Johnstons watching Matthew?" Dad asked.

"Mmm-hmm. He was thrilled that he didn't have to come to the specialist today."

Matthew's clinic was far away. I didn't recognize any of the neighborhoods we were driving through. For some reason, that gave me the creeps.

Dad jabbed me. "You're way too quiet, Vickie. Say something."

"I'm trying to imagine what the clinic will be like."

He lifted his eyebrows questioningly.

"I bet it's a tower made from poured concrete," I continued. "Blah. Gray. There's one rattly elevator to take people to the twenty-first floor. A lady in a white nurse's uniform meets patients. 'So,' she says, tapping a club in her palm, 'You're the family of Matthew Mahoney.' Then she takes us to the back where we're interrogated for hours before being released."

"Now you're making me nervous."

It was a joke, but the more I thought about it, the more scared I got. "This lady's not going to make me take a test or anything, is she?" I asked, finally. "To see if learning problems run in the family? Because if she does, I'll flunk for sure. I'm terrible at tests. I just flunked my math exam." As Mom's eye got huge, I hastily added, "That's just an expression, Mom. It means I didn't do all that great. A 'B' or something."

Normally she would have wanted all the details—

why I did poorly, how I could do better in the future. But she just sat back and squinted through the foggy windshield. She was preoccupied, all right.

"And worst of all," I said, letting the indignity in my heart swell up until it hurt, "Matthew and his learning disability are wrecking Christmas!"

We didn't talk the rest of the way to the clinic.

The specialist wasn't exactly scary.

Her nameplate said Jane Mulholland, and she stood up when we all crowded into her office. She was big, and her high heels made her seem like a giant.

"Finally we meet," she said to me, shaking my hand briskly. Her gray suit was businesslike and impressive, but her style was low-key. As soon as she got back to her desk she slipped off the jacket.

Mostly she wanted to talk about Matthew and his schoolwork. While Dad was telling how *he* had had problems in spelling and math as a kid, Mrs. Mulholland sneaked a stick of gum. I saw her take it out of the wrapper and pop it in her mouth. Every once in a while she took a little chew. Very discreet.

My aching neck started to relax. I leaned back in the chair and crossed my legs. This wasn't such a bad place. There was even a bowl of goldfish on the table behind her. One fish treaded water and stared at me. His orange tail swished. He made kissy faces at me with his lips.

Then she asked me some questions, like how did we get along and stuff. I told her how Matthew had made fun of my TV interview and how he was disorganized and forgetful. She just nodded and didn't act surprised at all. I thought maybe she would have said, "What a crummy thing to say about your brother. Shame on you!" But she didn't.

Finally we were talked out.

"Well," said the specialist. She leaned back in her swivel chair and folded her hands over her stomach, as if she had just finished an enormous lasagne dinner. "Everything sounds typical at the Mahoney house."

"Typical?" I said. I spoke softly but my voice shrilled up high like a bird. Typical was hotdish in the oven. Typical was Saturday cartoons and parents who went to PTA meetings. Typical was *not* first graders who couldn't even remember their ABCs.

Mrs. Mulholland nipped at her gum, chewing in time with the goldfish's kissing lips.

"That sounds funny, doesn't it? But your family situation *is* typical among children with learning differences."

"But," said Mom, "won't it ever get better?"

"Yes, of course. But not by itself. Sometimes medication helps. At any rate, this will take a lot of work and a lot of understanding."

"I'm nice to Matthew," I said. "I try to be patient. I try to be a good sister. But he acts so *weird*. He acts like a little brat most of the time."

Mrs. Mulholland leaned forward and rested her chin on her clasped hands. She had great eye contact, that's for sure.

"Vickie," she said. "Look at it from Matthew's point of view. Right now you're the star of the family. You get all the attention, and no matter how hard he tries, he just seems to get into trouble." She paused. "I'd be jealous and frustrated, too."

My heart gave itself a little pinch. I tried to imagine what it would be like to be thought of as a dumb kid instead of the one who wrote the winning $125-essay. And I had said mean things. To my own brother. I knew God would forgive me. But would Matthew?

"Don't look so heartsick, Vickie," Mrs. Mulholland interrupted, and gave a burbly laugh—like spaghetti sauce cooking on the stove. It was such a nice laugh that I couldn't help smiling, too. Pretty soon all of us were grinning. Mrs. Mulholland said: "None of this is anybody's fault."

You could practically see the relief on Mom and Dad's face.

I had an idea. "I could help him study," I said. "After school. I'm crummy in math, but I'm at least medium-smart in most everything else—"

I glanced over at my parents to see if they liked the idea. Both of them looked a little stunned, as if everyone they knew had just jumped out from behind the furniture and yelled "Surprise!" It was probably the way I had looked when Mr. Brownsdale called me up to the Keats auditorium stage.

Mrs. Mulholland rapped her desk with her fingers. Finally she said, "Vickie, your willingness to help is a giant step forward. But Matthew's diagnostic tests showed that he has trouble remembering. Memorizing is a real problem for children with learning differences. So just studying with Matthew isn't going to correct the situation. We need a new plan of attack. A whole new system."

She shuffled a few papers around and finally found her glasses. Then she sat up straight, her hands folded. She looked as though she might be guarding a secret under them. "Now," she said, showing large teeth that were a little crooked. "Let's talk about some ways you can help."

21

Dad came bursting through Matthew's bedroom door. "What's the trouble in here?"

Matthew and I looked up at him and blinked.

"You two are fighting again, aren't you?" he demanded. "I keep hearing these wild whoops and shouts. What's going on?"

"Dad," I said calmly. "We're not fighting. We're studying."

"Studying?" He crossed his arms and looked around the room uncertainly. "Since when do people have to scream and holler to study?"

My brother, who was sitting cross-legged on the bed across from me, spoke up. "It's a new system. Vickie made it up."

I couldn't help smiling at Dad's shocked face. I was feeling pretty proud of my system.

"Mrs. Mulholland said to repeat and repeat, right?" I said. "And to make studying interesting?"

Dad took a seat on the edge of the bed. "Right."

"That's what we're trying to do. Right, Matthew?"

"Right, Vickie."

"Okay," said Dad, beginning to show the signs of a smile. "Let's see it."

"Ready?" I said to Matthew.

"Ready."

I whipped out a flash card. It was a big square piece of cardboard. The letter C was printed in my somewhat sloppy handwriting on one side. "Go ahead," I said. "Name that letter!"

"It's a C!" he shouted.

"Right!"

Together we both leaped off the bed, shrieking and stomping our feet. Then, quietly, we climbed back up on the bedspread and took our positions.

"Okay," I said. "Part 2. Name three words that begin with C." I pointed at him. "Go."

"Cow," said my brother. He paused, screwing up his face.

I waited. There was no time limit in my new system.

"Cat," he said finally. He thought hard again. "Cocoa-Krispies!" he shouted triumphantly.

Dad looked at me, then at Matthew, then back at

me. "That's quite a system, Victoria."

"It's fun," said Matthew, bouncing up and down. "I don't know *all* the letters, but I know some of 'em. Mr. Crawford's going to be surprised." Suddenly his face drooped. "Vickie, what if I forget? I'll probably forget my letters again. I always do."

"We'll just keep practicing," I told him. "Pretty soon they'll be in cement. In your memory, that is. Don't be such a worry wart."

"Worry wart, worry wart," he sang, falling backwards on the bed and laughing hysterically.

Downstairs the phone rang, and in a second Mom's voice called up, "Vickie, phone call for you!"

I told Matthew he was excused to play. Then I rushed downstairs.

Whenever the phone rings, I always get this pang of excitement. I don't know why. Maybe I think some guy is going to call or something, though very few boys have called me in the past.

"It's just me," said Chelsie when I said hello.

I started to explain about Matthew and the clinic and Mrs. Mulholland, but my words came out so fast they seemed jumbled, and anyway I wasn't sure if Chelsie was following me. I guess if you don't have a kid with learning differences in your family, it's hard to imagine what it's like.

But she seemed interested; at least she said, "Uh huh" a lot. She waited until I was done, and then she said: "Two things. First, have you ever heard of 'love from afar'?"

I thought for a second. "Is it a song?"

"No, it's something Peg has. She says it's the kind of love she feels for that Julian Chandler guy who interviewed you on TV." Her voice deepened. "Now, listen to this. She called him up on the phone and talked to him for half an hour!"

"You're kidding!"

"Would I make that up? She actually called him up. Probably she only talked to him for fifteen minutes. Peg never can tell the straight truth."

I settled back on the stair steps, prepared for a good story.

". . . Anyway, after seeing him on TV, she decided she had to meet him. Plus she wanted his autograph or something. Peg is wild about celebrities. So she called him up and told him she was doing a social studies report about broadcast journalism."

"She's not doing a social studies report about broadcast journalism," I pointed out.

"I know that," said Chelsie. "But now she says she's in 'love from afar.' Can you believe it? Only Peggy." She sighed. "That's my story number one. Want to hear my story number two? It's really a question."

"What?"

"Here it is: do you want to hear my Vic Mahoney Promotion Plan for the new year? I've outlined my ideas." She giggled. "Some of them are pretty wild."

A couple of weeks ago, I would have wanted to hear all the plans. I might even have halfway be-

113

lieved that Chelsie could get me on TV in L.A. or New York. But suddenly I didn't want to play along anymore, not really. Johnny Carson wasn't going to interview a kid just because she had written a good essay. It was just me, Victoria Mahoney, not some superstar.

I opened my mouth to tell Chelsie, but then I closed it again. Probably she didn't want to hear it, and anyway she probably already knew it herself.

"Maybe you could come over tomorrow night and tell me," I offered. "As a First-Day-of-Vacation-It's-Almost-Christmas celebration."

"Love it. A sleep-over?"

"I'll ask." I put down the phone and went to find Mom and Dad.

I located them in the family room, and they said yes immediately. They're pretty generous about stuff like that, and not too fussy about messing up the house. I flew back to the telephone.

"Tomorrow," I said. "My place."

"Gotcha."

We said our usual "see you tomorrows" and hung up.

I went back to the family room, where my parents were measuring windows for new curtains. Matthew and I had already picked out fabric—a black background with tiny yellow TV screens. We thought it was hilarious.

"Is this the girl who's been helping her brother study?" asked Mom. She stretched to reach the measuring tape up.

"Right," I said. "That's me."

"Well, bless your heart," she said. The look she gave me made me feel warm.

I put my hand on my hip and lowered my eyelids. "Don't mention it, I'm sure, Mrs. Mahoney," I said in a fake sophisticated voice.

Without warning, Mom laughed. She hooted. She laughed so hard she dropped the measuring tape. Dad and I just stared at her in amazement. But pretty soon she had us laughing and gripping our sides, too.

"Boy," she said, finally. "I could use some of that every once in a while. I haven't had a good laugh in ages."

"Really?" I said. "You haven't heard the one about the fisherman and the big-mouthed bass?"

"As a matter of fact," she said, beginning to grin again. "I haven't. Tell me all about it."

22

It was starting to snow when Kristie, Janell, Chels, and I rushed outside after school. Free!

As we walked along the sidewalk, Janell sang a verse of "I'm Dreaming of a White Christmas." Some boys waiting for their bus sang along in high, silly voices and wiggled their hips and followed behind us. If it had been me, I probably would have clammed up, but Janell just bellowed louder to drown them out. We all laughed and walked on.

When we came to the corner where we split up, we stopped.

"I love snow at Christmas," said Peg. "I'm from Mississippi, and it *never* snows in Mississippi."

We rolled our eyes. We all know where Peg is

from, but she's always telling us, like it's news.

"I love Christmas, period," said Kristie. "It puts me in a good mood. I'm even nice to my brother this time of year."

Chelsie shook her head. "Your poor brother. You always say terrible things about him. I've met him, and I don't think he's so bad."

Kristie thought it over. "You're right. My New Year's resolution will be to treat my brother decently. I won't say one crummy thing about him all year." She paused. "There's just one problem. I never keep my New Year's resolutions."

We hung around for a while, talking about our vacation plans. Then we all headed off, waving and yelling, "Merry Christmas."

Chels and I went home the long way, so she could stop at her house and pick up her pajamas and stuff. The snow was coming down heavy and wet. With her head coated in snow, Chels looked like an old white-haired woman. I don't know what I looked like, but Chels kept looking at me and grinning.

At my house, the phone was ringing. I charged in to answer it. It was Mom.

"I'm going to be late," she told me. "Start dinner, will you?"

Normally I would have moaned. My parents know I'm no good at cooking. But with Chelsie around, everything was different. "Sure," I said.

"There's some money in the kitty," she said, referring to an old soup can we kept in the cupboard.

"Run to the store and buy ingredients for pizza."

"Pizza?" I said in amazement.

"Vegetarian, of course," she said. "Buy red and green peppers. That will look Christmasy. By the way, Matthew's with you, isn't he?"

"He's right here," I said, glancing over at my brother. He and Chelsie were pulled up at the kitchen table rolling flourescent clay into long skinny ropes.

"How's he behaving?"

"So far, so good. Don't worry, Mom."

"Okay." Mom sounded relieved. "Thanks for taking care of things. I'll see you guys in a couple of hours. Dad's coming home tonight, too."

"Great!"

"So long."

I made a list of items (including carob-covered peanuts for the empty candy bowl), and we started off.

Matthew was acting pretty crazy. He kept dashing ahead like, pretending he was going to run out into the street. I couldn't even carry on a regular conversation with Chelsie.

"For the last time," I finally called to him, "be careful!" He stopped and looked at me, and his face looked funny. It was puzzled, as if he wasn't sure whether he should pitch a fit or ignore me or what. In a calmer voice, I added: "You're the only brother I've got, you know."

It was weird. His face sort of relaxed. After that

he slowed down and dawdled along, just a few steps ahead of us.

" 'You're the only brother I've got'?" Chels had pulled a cap over her sopping hair, and the oval of her face was white and surprised. "Wow. Pure mush."

I felt my face beginning to burn up. "It's true," I mumbled. "Isn't it?"

She was quiet for awhile. Then she said softly, "What you said was nice, Vic. No, really, I mean it."

"Matthew's okay," I said, embarrassed.

We crunched along in silence, and in the soft haze of snow, the world seemed fresh and beautiful and new. A prayer formed suddenly in my head. *Thank you, God. I'm not exactly sure for what. Just everything, I guess.*

Even before I had finished thinking it, I had this idea, and it was a powerful feeling that wiped out the cold. God loved me. He really did. No matter what I did, or how I disappointed Him, or whether or not I won writing contests, or whether I was popular or a celebrity. He was always right there, loving me. That's one great thing about God. He doesn't play favorites. To Him, I was lovable just exactly the way I was. And Matthew, I realized, was lovable too—even with his learning disability.

We walked along. Up ahead, my brother was rolling a perfectly round ball of snow. He patted it with his small mittens and grinned back at us.

"I admire you for being no nice to Matthew," Chelsie said. She paused and turned to look at me. The edges of her smirk were just visible above the edge of her scarf. "Maybe, just maybe, old 'Flashy-Smile' Chandler was right about you. Maybe you really are a sweetheart."

I held up my fist like I was going to give her a bonk, but she had already taken off. We ran the rest of the way to the store.

23

Matthew tromped into the kitchen. "Eccckk. What's that smell?"

At the stove, Dad continued stirring. "A great delicacy."

I had been hanging around for the last half hour, leaning on the counter and watching Dad cook, and I hadn't even noticed what he was making. I leaned over the pot. It was a milky liquid, with patches of floating melted butter. "What is it?"

"—a delight to the palate and the tongue."

"But what *is* it, Dad?"

"—one of the world's culinary masterpieces, a bouquet of simplicity and—"

"*Dad! What are you making?*"

"Oyster stew." The wooden spoon tapped gently against the pot as he stirred. "Oh, take those pained looks off your faces. This tastes a whole lot better than it sounds."

Matthew's nose wrinkled. "I just hope it tastes better than it *smells*," he said.

"My mother used to cook up a batch of oyster stew every Christmas Eve," Dad said, peppering the mixture. "It's an old family tradition. You kids could stand a little tradition. A few more years of this, you'll get used to the smell. You might even learn to like the wrinkly grey things you'll find in the bottom of your bowl."

"Dad—" I said, the horror beginning to dawn. "You don't mean—?"

"Yes." He crouched down like Quasimodo, cackling an evil laugh. "*Oysters!*"

Matthew took off. We heard him in the family room, making gagging noises. They sounded very realistic.

Sleepy and warm, I leaned on my elbows. Outside the snow was blowing, but here inside Dad was stirring, stirring, stirring, and Mom and Matthew were nearby, and life seemed pretty nice. Not perfect, but nice. Christmas Eve always feels good.

We heard Mom's footsteps on the back stairs, and then she came into the kitchen. She was dressed to the hilt. She had on her ritzy black velvet top, a swirly skirt, and some sparkly gold earrings.

Dad whistled. "What's the occasion?"

"You said you were making something special. I thought I'd dress for dinner." She cocked her ear. Matthew was still at it in the family room. "Ahh," she said. "The sounds of a normal happy family."

"Our kids don't appreciate my attempts to expand their culinary horizons, Bob," Dad told her.

She peered into the pot. "Oooo. Do you blame them? I mean, oyster stew, for goodness' sake. Don't tell me you liked oysters when you were a kid."

"Hated 'em."

"I thought so. Fortunately I've already made some delectable side courses. We can all fill up on *good* stuff." Mom winked at me. "I hate oysters, too."

Dad sighed. "I'm crushed." But he didn't stop stirring.

"As far as moms go," I said, hopping off the stool and giving her a hug, "you're a dream."

We unloaded stuff from the refrigerator together. Then Mom said, "Isadora and Harold will be here any minute, Vickie. Would you mind lighting candles?"

I went from room to room snapping a match to each wick. When I was done, the whole house glowed.

I came back into the kitchen, humming "God Rest Ye Merry, Gentlemen." "Let's put on a record—" I started. Then I stopped.

Mom and Dad were in a clinch. Maybe they couldn't help themselves, with the romantic candlelight and all. The oyster stew was probably burning up.

"Don't interrupt," Mom said, not opening her eyes.

I pulled up a chair and waited.

"So much for privacy," Dad said huffily, going back to his cooking. But he threw a smile at me over one shoulder. "You're a good kid, even if you can't leave us in peace for two seconds. Want to tell her the big news, Bobbi?"

They stood there grinning at each other for a few seconds. Finally Mom said, "Okay." She turned to me. "Are you good at keeping secrets?"

I was all ears. "Sure."

"Here goes. What's pudgy and cute and cries in the night? Guess quick, because we may soon have one around the house."

"You're going to have a baby?" I yelped. "When?"

She shook her head. "We're going to *get* a baby, not *have* one."

They can be very mysterious at times. I stared at their smiling faces. "I don't get it."

"It's simple," Dad said. "We're going to adopt a baby."

My mouth was glued shut. I couldn't say a word. Not one. I was speechless.

Mom went on. "A lot of kids don't have homes. And we have a good one—even though it always needs fixing up. For sure we have plenty of love and all that mushy stuff to go around.

"Plus, adoption would be the perfect solution for us. There's no guarantee that we wouldn't have the same problems again we had with Jessica. This way, we won't have to go through another nine months of worry. It'll take a while for all this to happen, and in the meantime we can work hard with Matthew."

"It's a great idea," I said. "It's a wonderful idea."

I was still a little numb with surprise, but a tingling excitement was already working its way into my fingertips. What would the baby look like? Would it be a girl or a boy? Red hair? Black? Would it like me?

"Mrs. Mulholland said we could tell your brother when it was definite. After we make some more progress with him, she's sure he can adjust."

Matthew came dashing in just then with a handful of envelopes. "Nobody brought the mail in today," he announced, and turned them over to Mom.

"Here," she said, pulling out an official-looking envelope and handing it to me. "Something for you."

When I saw the return address, I didn't have to rip it open to know what was inside. It was the check from the writing contest. I pulled out the crisp printed form. "One hundred twenty-five dollars and no/100----------" it said, and it was made out to Victoria Mahoney.

"Let's see, let's see, let's see!" said Matthew, jumping up and down. He got up close. His nose was practically touching the paper. "Wow," he said, breathing out.

I passed it around the room.

"Have you thought about what you're going to do with it?" Dad asked, going back to his cooking.

I shrugged. You can't just decide stuff like that on the spot. You have to roll it around awhile, thinking about ideas. For sure, though, I wanted to share some of it with Matthew. I wasn't even sure why I wanted to, I just did.

"Guess I'll go upstairs and change," I said. "This being a special occasion and all."

I trudged upstairs. The air got cooler as I went, as if I were climbing up a mountain. I kept going, feeling good, just plain good.

JUST VICTORIA

I am absolutely *dreading* junior high.

Vic and her best friend, Chelsie, have heard enough gory details about seventh grade to ruin their entire summer vacation. And as if school weren't a big enough worry, Vic suddenly finds problems at every turn:

• Chelsie starts hanging around Peggy Hiltshire, queen of all the right cliques, who thinks life revolves around the cheerleading squad.

• Vic's mom gets a "fulfilling" new job—with significantly less pay—at a nursing home.

• Grandma Warden is looking tired and pale—and won't see a doctor.

But Victoria Hope Mahoney has a habit of underestimating her own potential. The summer brings a lot of change, but Vic is equal to it as she learns more about her faith, friendship, and growing up.

Don't miss any books in
The Victoria Mahoney Series!

SHELLY NIELSEN lives in Minneapolis, Minnesota, with her husband and two Yorkshire terriers.

MORE VICTORIA

Suddenly, life is nothing but problems.

Vic can see that there will be nothing dull about seventh grade . . . if she can only survive it.

First, there are the anonymous notes saying Corey Talbott, the rowdiest and most popular guy in the seventh grade has a crush on *her*. It's ridiculous, of course. But who could be writing them? And what will Vic do if Corey finds out?

Then, thanks again to the mysterious note sender, Victoria gets sent to the principal's office—the first time in her life she's faced such humiliation. What will her parents say? The last thing they need is one more thing to argue about . . . .

Live the ups and downs of Vic's first months of junior high in *More Victoria*.

Don't miss any books in
The Victoria Mahoney Series!

SHELLY NIELSEN lives in Minneapolis, Minnesota, with her husband and two Yorkshire terriers.

TAKE A BOW, VICTORIA

I might as well die of embarrassment right here.

Victoria is finding plenty to cringe about these days, such as her hugely pregnant mom waddling into the school auditorium in full view of all Vic's friends. (Couldn't she sit quietly at home till the baby arrives?) Or such as Isadora, her flashy grandmother, actually volunteering as set designer for the spring production at school. (Couldn't she bake cookies and knit like a normal grandma?)

Meanwhile Vic is struggling with her own confusing wish to be a star . . . and to stay safely hidden backstage. As some important events change life for the Mahoney family, Vic finds her ideas of stardom—and of courage—changing, too.

Don't miss any books in The Victoria Mahoney Series!

#1 Just Victoria   #4 Only Kidding, Victoria

#2 More Victoria   #5 Maybe It's Love, Victoria

#3 Take a Bow, Victoria   #6 Autograph, Please,
                           Victoria

SHELLY NIELSEN lives in Minneapolis, Minnesota, with her husband and two Yorkshire terriers.

ONLY KIDDING, VICTORIA

You've got to be kidding!

Spend the summer at a resort lodge in Minnesota . . . with her *family?* When she's been looking forward to endless days of good times with her new friends from school?

Victoria can't believe her parents are serious, but nothing she can do or say will change their minds. It's off to Little Raccoon Lake, a nowhere place where she's sure there will be nothing to do.

But the summer holds a lot of surprises—like Nina, one year older and a whole lot tougher, who scoffs at rules . . . and at Vic for bothering to keep them. And the bittersweet pang that comes with each letter from her best friend, Chelsie, reminding Vic of what she's missing back home. But the biggest surprise is Victoria's discovery of some things that have been right under her nose all along . . . .

Don't miss any books in
The Victoria Mahoney Series!

SHELLY NIELSEN lives in Minneapolis, Minnesota, with her husband and two Yorkshire terriers.

MAYBE IT'S LOVE VICTORIA

Love is mysterious.

"You never know when love is going to walk up and bop you right in the head." That's what Vic's best friend, Chelsie, says, and Chelsie usually knows. And Vic has plenty of other "mysteries" to puzzle over, too, the fall she enters eighth grade.

• How can she help Chels, who has (finally) become a Christian and expects all their friends to see and care about the big change in her life?

• How can she keep her crazy grandmother's wedding from becoming a three-ring circus (complete with a bridesmaid's dress that makes Vic look like a bumblebee)?

• And how is she supposed to figure out this crazy thing called love?

Vic's faith in God grows as together she and Chelsie weather another season of junior high.

Don't miss any books in The Victoria Mahoney Series!

#1 Just Victoria   #4 Only Kidding, Victoria

#2 More Victoria   #5 Maybe It's Love, Victoria

#3 Take a Bow, Victoria   #6 Autograph, Please, Victoria

SHELLY NIELSEN lives in Minneapolis, Minnesota, with her husband and two Yorkshire terriers.